A Fictional Detective Trifecta

~ Novellas Featuring
the
Fictional Detective ~

By Greg Fowlkes

Includes a Bonus Story from the book

Trial by Magic

~ Tales from the Casebook of The Wizard at Law ~

and a Sneak Preview from the book

Star City Stories

Space Opera Noir
Featuring Frank Sladek, P.I.

A Fictional Detective Trifecta

Published by Intrepid Ink, LLC

Intrepid Ink, LLC provides full publishing services to authors of fiction and non-fiction books, eBooks and websites. From editing to formatting, to publishing, to marketing, Intrepid Ink gets your creative works into the hands of the people who want to read them.

Find out more at www.IntrepidInk.com.

ISBN 13: 978-1-937022-97-6

Printed in the United States of America

Books by Greg Fowlkes

From the Wizard at Law Series:

The Laws of Magic
Trial by Magic

From the Murder on Mars Series:

Blood Red Sands of Mars
A Death at Station Alpha
A Corpse in Hut Town
Murder at the Mars Club

From the Fictional Detective Series:

The Fictional Detective
A Fictional Detective Trifecta

Star City Stories: Space Opera Noir Featuring Frank Sladek

The Uncorrupted Corpse

Tequila Visions

Cargo From Paradise

Ice Viking

About the Author

Greg Fowlkes is a writer, musician and programmer. He obtained a Master's degree in Physics from the University of Wisconsin. Currently he lives outside of Madison, Wisconsin, with his partner Irene and two Shiba Inu dogs named respectively after a samurai actor (Toshiro) and one of that actor's more famous roles (Yojimbo). When not walking dogs, he enjoys reading, making craftsman furniture and playing the guitar and mandolin. His latest musical project is learning the playing style of gypsy jazz guitarist Django Reinhardt. Greg's series of books include The Murder on Mars series, The Wizard at Law series, and The Fictional Detective series.

Table Of Contents

The Fictional Detective Speaks with the Dead

The Fictional Detective Speaks with the Dead

My name is Frank Slade. I'm a private detective. At least I think I am. Oh, I'm sure I'm a private dick, but some things about my last case have caused me to question my reality. I'm a man without a past. Before a few months ago there's nothing to prove I ever existed, no paper trail, no public record. My own memories from that time are all kind of vague and hazy. And generic, like they were details created by someone making them up. Like maybe someone named Ezekial O. Handler, the mystery writer that got bumped off not too long ago by his publisher. Oh, there are a few people who claim to have known me, like Flannigan, a police detective, but when I checked into it, his past is no more substantial than my own. Handler wrote me a letter in which he claimed he was responsible, that he had created me to avenge his death by means of some spell he had gotten out of an old book, just like he had created Flannigan, Armand the ex-jockey who operates a newsstand downstairs, a female impersonator named Josephine LaTouche, and Janet Nielsen, my fiancée and Handler's old girl friend. It was a pretty wild claim, even if it did seem to fit the evidence. But Handler had proved to have a good idea of the events that followed his death. If I were a thinking man, it might have bothered me, wondering whether I was real or not, but I'm just a simple private gumshoe and the whole thing is just too existential to worry about.

The current reality is that I'm a private detective with an office in a low rent building in a not particularly nice part of town. The office is what you'd expect would come out of the imagination of a mystery writer known more for his lurid titles than his high literary style. Of course, it's also just the sort of office a not terribly successful P.I. might rent. There's the frosted glass in the door with my name in peeling black paint, the second hand furniture, the bottle of bourbon stashed in the desk drawer. It's the kind of office that you've seen at the start of a dozen mystery movies and read about in more pulp thrillers than you can count. I won't describe it in detail, you can visualize it perfectly without really trying.

Like I said, I'm a private dick, though my fiancée is trying to get me to quit. It's too dangerous she says, and after Handler left her the rights to his last book, the one published after he was killed, it's not like we're going to need the money. She says I should try my hand at writing, detective fiction stuff, says I'd be a natural at it, and wit the Handler connection I'd have no problem finding a publisher. What the heck. I might as well give it a try, so here goes. This is an account of my most recent case as it actually happened. It might even be real.

I was sitting in my office going through my files. This was a couple of weeks after I'd solved the Handler murder. That case had left me with a lot of unanswered questions about the nature of reality and I'd gone into a kind of funk that ended up in a week-long drunk. After I'd sobered up I came to the conclusion that no matter what the truth was, there was nothing I could do about it and I might as well just get on with life. After all, it wasn't shaping up as such a bad life. Janet and I were talking about getting married. Janet is the kind of dame men dream about; tall, good looking with curves in all the right places. She was smart and had money, too. We'd be fixed for life with what Handler had left her in his will.

I was thinking about getting out of the business, and was trying to tie up loose ends. I wasn't really looking for any new cases, but I was still listed in the phone book and business directory and it still said "Private Detective" under my name on the frosted glass in the office door. I wasn't completely surprised then, when there came a tentative knock on that door. It was a woman's knock, quick, light, not so much demanding attention as imploring for it.

I stood up, stashed the bottle of bourbon and the glass in the bottom drawer and went to open the door. The last time I had done that, the woman had been Janet, a leggy blonde with looks straight out of a fashion magazine. My visitor was nothing like that.

She was a big woman, not fat, but ample, probably in her mid fifties. She was dressed expensively in a dress and coat that actually fit her and made her seem thinner than she really was. Her hair had been styled recently in one of those cuts that women who can afford it wear. She reminded me as much as anything of the heavy set broad who always played the older rich dame in the Marx brothers movies. You know the one I mean, the one who never seemed to get the jokes.

"Mr. Slade?" she asked tentatively.

"That's me. What can I do for you?"

"I believe you are a—a private detective?"

"That's what it says on the door, though I'm thinking of getting out of the racket."

"Oh—I'm sorry. I thought—" I could see she had trouble on her mind. I never could turn down a dame in trouble, even an older one.

"Please, come in. The least I can do is hear your story. After all, you came all this way down here to talk to me."

"That's very kind, Mr. Slade." She entered the office and took the chair facing the desk. Despite her size she moved with a certain kind of grace. I shut the office door and sat in my desk chair.

When I was seated she said, "I don't quite know where to start."

"Why don't we start with the simple things. Like your name."

"Yes. Of course. I'm Geraldine DuVille. My husband was Herbert DuVille. He ran a trucking business, Tri-State Transportation Services, until he died recently."

"My condolences, Mrs. DuVille. Just what did you want to consult with me about?"

"Well, it's like this, Mr. Slade. Some time before his death, my husband took on some partners. He needed some capital to expand the business."

"How was the business doing, if you don't mind my asking?"

"Quite well, I think. I never bothered too much about the business. I left that to Herbert. But we had always lived quite comfortably. Herbert was a good provider." I could hear the love in her voice. "I'm not sure why Herbert felt the need to expand, but he seemed to think it was important."

"And these partners he brought on? Were they on the up and up?"

"They seemed to be at first. They were just going to invest some money and leave the running of the business to my husband. But after awhile they wanted to become more involved. He never said anything about it, but I could tell that Herbert wasn't altogether happy with the situation."

"Any particulars?"

"As I said, Mr. Slade, I never involved myself with the business. And then Herbert died, and that changed everything."

"Just how did he die?"

"An accident, or so I thought—"

"But something has caused you to change your mind?"

"I'm getting to that. The arrangement as I understand it was that my husband retained fifty-one percent of the company while Mr. McClure and Mr. Trentino split the remainder of the shares between them. However, there appears to have been an unfortunate clause placed in the contract by which they invested. In the event of the death of any of the partners, their share of the company would be split between the surviving partners. The result was that when my husband died his share of the company went to Mr. McClure and Mr. Trentino, and I was left with nothing."

"Your husband didn't leave anything to you?"

"Oh, no, Mr. Slade. I don't want you to think that. He left me the house, of course and some investments. There was also a large insurance policy that he had taken out shortly after we were married. I don't want you to think that he left me a pauper. I may not be able to live quite as well as before, but I shall get by. But it's the thought of the company that Herbert worked so hard to build just going to those— others that bothers me."

"You've talked to a lawyer about this, haven't you?"

"Yes. He said that it was an unusual agreement, but it seemed perfectly legal. He didn't hold out much hope for litigation, I'm afraid."

"I'm sorry about your troubles, Mrs. DuVille, but I'm not quite sure what it is you want me to do?"

"What I want you to do, Mr. Slade is come to a séance."

"A séance?" I said with surprise. It was about the last thing I had expected.

"Yes, a séance, Mr. Slade. I know that this may sound to you like a strange request, but I have been in touch with my husband, and he wishes to speak with you personally. There is something that he wants to tell you."

"You've talked to your husband? At a séance?"

"Yes."

"And he asked for me?" I couldn't keep the skepticism out of my voice.

"Yes. He was quite particular about that point. At the last session he asked for you. That's why I came down here, Mr. Slade. I assure you that I don't normally employ private detectives."

"I didn't think you did, Mrs. DuVille. I admit that I have very little experience with these kind of things, but isn't this an awfully specific request for someone who is dead to communicate."

"I assure you, Mr. Slade, that this séance was not a silly parlor game like those Ouija boards. The Professor is a very serious person."

"The professor?"

"Yes, the medium. Professor Longwell. He's quite well known, Mr. Slade."

"I'm sure he is." Probably by half the bunko squads in the state, I thought to myself.

"I detect a note of doubt, Mr. Slade, but I am willing to pay you for your time, whatever your standard rate is. Please, won't you come? I'm a desperate woman." She seemed on the point of tears.

"It's a hundred dollars a day. Plus expenses."

"What's a hundred dollars?"

"That's my standard fee, Mrs. DuVille. When is this séance?"

"Tonight, if you can make it. I'm sure I can arrange it with the Professor. He's been so helpful."

"I'm sure he has. As it is, I am available tonight. What time?"

"Would nine o'clock be possible?"

"That shouldn't be a problem." Janet was going to fix me dinner, but we'd be done in plenty of time.

"Fine. Here's the address," she handed me a card with her name and address.

"Tonight, then. And don't worry, you can pay me after the séance."

"Thank you, Mr. Slade. I'll be waiting for you."

She rose and I escorted her to the door.

After she left, I thought about the deal. Was she just some poor widow being preyed upon by a charlatan? Or was there more to this séance business? I didn't really believe in ghosts. On the other hand, I didn't not believe in them either. I'd seen enough strange things lately to keep an open mind. Of anyone in the world, I was the last to question the reality of such things. Or the reality of anything, for that matter.

I remembered reading about Herbert DuVille's death in the papers, but couldn't recall any of the details. It hadn't made much of a splash, just a few column inches in the financial section. The death had been ruled an accident. A jewelry heist the next day that had left two dead had pretty much seized my attention along with that of just about everyone else in town.

I decided to give my favorite flat-foot a call. He worked the homicide squad, and if there was anything about DuVille's death that hadn't made the papers, he'd be the one to know.

The phone rang three or four times before a voice announced, "Homicide, Lt. Flannigan." He didn't sound happy. Like he wasn't getting enough sleep.

"It's Frank. Got a minute?"

"Oh, sure, Frank. I've got plenty of time for cheap private dicks. After all, that's what we're here for, isn't it?"

"I can sense that you're busy, so I'll make it quick. What do you know about Herbert DuVille's death?"

"DuVille? It was ruled an accident. Some boxes fell on him at his warehouse or something like that. Why the interest?"

"His widow was just in my office. Apparently her husband has something he wants to tell me."

"Her husband, huh? Wait a minute. Is this some kind of gag, Slade? Her husband's dead."

"It's no gag, Flannigan. Or if it is, it's on me. She wants me to attend a séance. She claims her husband is going to communicate with me from beyond."

"Beyond what?"

"You got me."

"You're not taking this seriously, are you Frank?"

"I don't know. Like I said, his widow was in my office wanting to hire me. She seemed kind of upset. The way I figure, it's probably some huckster trying to take advantage of a poor widow that just happens to have some money. I thought I'd go to this séance and maybe find the hidden wires or whatever."

Flannigan said, "I thought you were thinking about getting out of the P.I. business, Frank."

"Yeah, I am. Janet doesn't like the idea of me putting myself in danger. But how much risk can there be at a séance?"

"I don't know, Frank. Some of these older dames can get some crazy ideas."

"I think I can protect myself. By the way, you wouldn't know anything about a Professor Longwell, would you?"

"Who's that?"

"He's the guy that's holding the séance. The medium."

"Not my line, Frank, but I can ask the guys in Bunko if they've ever heard of him."

"That would be swell, Flannigan. I'll be at Janet's until about 8:30."

"A hot dame like that, and you want to run around messing with ghosts. If you ask me, you're the crazy one, Frank."

"I get that a lot. Let me know if you find out anything. I'll let you get back to your corpses, Flannigan."

I found myself talking to a dead phone. Flannigan had cause for being short of patience. He had been putting in long hours working the jewelry heist murders. A salesclerk and the store's owner had been found dead. Over a million in prime ice was missing, too, without much in the way of clues.

I looked at the clock on the wall. It was getting late, and Janet was expecting me for dinner. I didn't want to disappoint her.

Janet lived in a swank apartment building on the east side. It was swank enough to have a doorman. He didn't approve of me despite the fact that I'd been coming around regularly since the Handler case. To mollify him I'd taken to parking my Chevy in front of the building next door. It didn't seem to make much difference. He still sneered snootily as he opened the door to let me in. I smiled and touched the brim of my hat.

"Thank you, George," I said brightly.

He acknowledged me icily, "Mr. Slade."

Janet still lived in the seven room apartment Handler had paid for when she had been his mistress. There was no good reason to move. The insurance money from his death had left her with more than enough to pay the rent. It had always been more her place than his, anyway. He'd lived in a creepy old mansion that had been built by one of the beer barons a century earlier. He'd left her that in his will as well, but both of us liked the apartment, better.

You wouldn't think a dame built like Janet would be able to cook. With her looks, you wouldn't think she'd have to. Tall, leggy, a natural blonde, she had a body that ran to just enough soft curves to it to keep a guy interested. But she also knew that the way to keep a man happy was through his stomach. I certainly wasn't complaining. I'd put five pounds on my lean frame since I'd become a regular guest.

I had a key to the front door, so I let myself in. She popped out of the kitchen to greet me along with the odors of cooking beef. She was wearing a grey skirt and a sweater just loose enough to look comfortable. She had on a cute little apron, too. Janet is one of the few women I know who can cook in spike heels and not look ridiculous. For that matter, she's one of the few women I know who can cook.

"You're on time, Frank," she said as she pecked my cheek. "Dinner will be ready in a few minutes. I'm just working on the sauce now. Why don't you pour us some wine."

I went into the dining room where there was a bottle of California Cabernet open on the table. I poured a few fingers into the waiting glasses.

"What's for dinner," I called into the kitchen.

"Filets with an au poivre sauce, Caesar salad, and baked potatoes," came the reply. Three months earlier, I hadn't known what an au poivre sauce was, the beef that I ate had the consistency of shoe leather and I had thought salad was for rabbits. There were candles on the table, too. Love can do wonders for a man's diet.

"Sounds great." I took a sip of the wine. To my embarrassment I realized I had swirled the glass and sniffed it beforehand. Old Ezekial's scripting of my character seemed to be unraveling.

Janet came out of the kitchen holding two plates, each with a filet covered in sauce. "Could you get the salad, Frank?"

Of course I could get the salad. I might be a lot of things, but crazy isn't one of them.

We didn't talk much during dinner. Jazz played softly on the stereo. If I'd been able to look at myself, I'd probably have been grinning like an idiot.

When I'd finished the last of the steak I said, "I have to go out tonight."

Janet looked at me with concern. "I thought you were getting out of the business, Frank."

"I am, baby. But this woman came into my office this afternoon. She'd recently lost her husband."

"Is this woman young?"

"Don't worry. She's about twice your age. Probably twice your weight, too." That seemed to mollify Janet a little.

"Will it be dangerous, Frank?"

"It shouldn't be. She wants me to attend a séance."

"A séance?" The note of concern was still in her voice. Maybe with good reason. Janet had as much cause to doubt her reality as I do mine.

"Yeah. To speak to her dead husband."

"Is that something you should be dealing with, Frank?" I'd never shown her the last letter from Handler, the one where he claimed that we were all, Janet, Flannigan and myself, the product of a spell the writer had worked when he had discovered he was going to be killed by his publisher. But she had seen the other passages he had written before his death, the ones that had predicted our every move while trying to solve his murder. It could, of course, all have been a coincidence, the product of the imagination of a writer going off the deep end. That was the sane way to treat it. But neither one of us was comfortable discounting the supernatural.

"It's probably just some con man's game, trying to fleece a few bucks off a grieving widow. I figure I'll maybe blow his act or at least put a little fear in him so he'll take a powder and leave the widow alone."

"That's sweet of you, Frank. You're sure that this widow isn't young and attractive?"

"Baby, even if she was, she couldn't hold a candle to you."

"You say the nicest things, Frank. Even if you don't mean half of them."

I was saved from having to respond by the ringing of the phone.

"I'm expecting a call from Flannigan," I said as I got up to answer it.

It was the lieutenant. "I checked with Bunko. Seems this Professor Longwell is more or less legit. He's mostly a stage magician. He puts on his act at clubs around town. Mostly the Blue Angel, which figures. He does private shows at peoples' homes, too. Charges for them, but never anything outrageous. Bunko has checked him out once or twice, but never found anything to charge him with. None of the people he's performed for have ever filed a complaint. Bunko didn't know anything about séances."

"Thanks for the dirt, Flannigan."

"Let me know if you find out anything different."

"Sure thing." I hung up.

So Longwell didn't have a record as a scam artist. That didn't mean a thing. I'd just have to go have a look for myself.

The address I'd been given was in one of the old suburbs. It was a neighborhood where the bankers and store owners had gone to build their houses in the '20's. It had avoided decline in the post war years and was still a desirable locale if not quite as fashionable as it once had been.

The house where Mrs. DuVille lived was from that era, a brick Tudor revival parked on a well-landscaped two acre lot. It wasn't exactly a mansion, but it was large enough to be comfortable.

I parked the Chevy out front. There was only one other car at the curb, a late model sedan. It didn't look like the kind of car that I envisioned the Professor driving. I walked up the curving stone walk to the arched topped front door and rang the bell.

A few seconds later the door was opened by a short Hispanic woman who looked to be in her mid-forties. She was neatly dressed and her accent was just discernible when she offered to take my hat. With my hat in hand she ushered me into a room just off the main hall. It had the look of a formal sitting room, furnished conservatively with what looked to be quality pieces. Everything was neat and spotless.

I noticed a photo on the mantelpiece above the fireplace. It was of Mrs. DuVille and a man I assumed was the late Herbert DuVille. He was a thin man, several inches shorter than his wife with thinning hair that he had combed over the top of his head. The pose was formal, but the two of them looked quite happy.

Along with Mrs. DuVille was another woman of about the same age if nowhere near the same size. The other woman, who Mrs. DuVille introduced as her friend Mrs. Johanssen, was dressed somewhat primly in not quite old lady style. She looked like a woman who could afford quality things but didn't spend money needlessly. There was no sign of Professor Longwell.

"I'm so glad you could make it, Mr. Slade. As you can see, we are still waiting for Professor Longwell. I'm expecting him any minute now."

As if on cue, the doorbell rang. A few moments later the maid, or housekeeper, I wasn't sure which, ushered in a man I immediately knew was Professor Longwell. He wasn't exactly what I had expected. A thin man, pushing sixty, he was dressed in a suit of conservative cut and color. The only thing that might lead one to think he was something other than an accountant or bank teller was the rather sharply pointed Van Dyke beard and curling moustaches, both of which were neat if a bit flamboyant.

"Professor, this is Mr. Slade. You remember that at the last session Herbert asked for him to be present?"

"Mr. Slade," he said acknowledging the introduction. He extended a hand with long, thin fingers that didn't look a bit effeminate. His grip was firm and precise when we shook. "I'm so glad that you could attend our séance tonight. Mr. DuVille was most particular about wishing to speak with you." His voice was that of someone used to speaking in public. It was neither low nor high in pitch, but steady. All the words were clearly enunciated like a radio announcer.

"I'm not sure what you all are expecting of me," I replied. "I've never participated in a séance before."

"It's really quite simple, Mr. Slade. The four of us will sit at the table here." There was a sort of card table that had been set up in the middle of the room. Four chairs were arranged, one on each side. "We will turn down the lights and hold hands and wait for the spirits to contact us. Of course, I can't guarantee that anything will occur, Mr. Slade. Communications with the spirit world is notoriously capricious."

"I have no particular expectations, professor. It's your show. I'm just here in a professional capacity."

He gave a little chuckle. "I am aware of that, Mr. Slade. If you have no further questions, then, shall we begin?"

The two ladies seemed to know the drill and sat in chairs facing each other, one to the east and one to the west. The professor indicated with a gesture of his hand that I should take the seat to the south. He waited until I had taken my place before he, too, sat down.

Mrs. DuVille then asked, "Esmeralda, would you turn off the lights, please?" the maid did as instructed without a word and then left the room, closing the French doors to the hallway behind her. The room wasn't quite in total darkness. Several candles had been lit on the fireplace mantel and a dim light shown through the fabric covering the windows in the French doors.

"Now, if you will each take the hand of the person next to you, we may begin," the professor requested.

I took Mrs. DuVille's hand in my right and Mrs. Johanssen's in my left. In the dim light, I could see the professor doing the same. I didn't see how he was going to bang a tambourine or whatever, at least with his hands, but then that was the trick with fake mediums. They kept their hands in clear view while working gimmicks with their knees and feet.

We waited that way for quite awhile, maybe five minutes. Surprisingly, there was no chanting on the part of the Professor, no sound effects, no theatrics of any sort. I was wondering if Mrs. DuVille was going to get her money's worth that night, or if the Professor had chosen to tamp things down on account of my presence.

I needn't have worried. Suddenly the candle flames wavered as if from a gust of wind and the temperature of the room seemed to drop several degrees. The Professor sat motionlessly across from me, his eyes closed as far as I could tell. Mrs. Johanssen shifted nervously in her seat. I looked around, seeing if I could spot the cause of the draft. The doors and windows were all tightly shut and I hadn't heard the sound of a furnace or air conditioner kicking in. I'd noticed, anyway, that the room was heated with radiators.

There was another few minutes of silence before a voice broke in. It was using the Professor's mouth, but the high, slightly squeaky voice didn't sound anything like the mellifluous tones of the magician. Mrs. DuVille gave a little shudder.

"Mr. Slade? Is that you?" the voice asked.

I looked at the Professor for some sign that I should answer, but he seemed to be in some sort of trance. I decided to take the chance. "I'm Slade."

"Thank you for coming. There is something I want you to do for me."

This wasn't what I had expected. There was no fading in and out like a bad radio signal, no barely discernible words. Instead, it was just like we were conducting a conversation across the table.

"What is it, Mr. DuVille? I assume it is Mr. Herbert DuVille that I'm speaking to?"

"I am Herbert DuVille, Mr. Slade. Or at least what remains of him."

"I'll accept that. Just what is it that you want me to do?"

"I'm warning you, Mr. Slade, it may be dangerous." I hadn't expected a ghost to be so concerned with my health.

"That's never stopped me before."

"Very well. I want you to go to Al's Barber Shop on the corner of Blake and Fennimore. Tell the owner that you are there to pick up something that was left for you. Tell him Ray Nitschke sent you."

For a ghost, Herbert seemed to have some sense of humor. I was starting to wonder if I was the butt of some joke being played on me. Maybe it was something Janet had cooked up to keep me out of trouble. I guess I could play along. After all, I was a Packer's fan, too.

"OK. Go to Al's Barber Shop on Blake and Fennimore. Say Ray Nitschke sent me for something. What do I do with it?"

"I think you'll be able to figure it out, Mr. Slade. Zeke said you were a sharp one, at least the way he wrote you." I was the one to shudder, then. Even in the spirit world Ezekial couldn't be that common a name. Was Handler still controlling my destiny?

"You've met Handler, there in the spirit world?" I asked. It didn't do me any good. Contact seemed to have been broken. The Professor's eyes were open and he had let go of the hands of Mrs. Slade and Mrs. Johanssen.

"I'm afraid this session is over, Mr. Slade," the professor said. "Were you successful in reaching Mr. DuVille?"

"You didn't hear?"

"I'm afraid that when I'm in a trance my mind is somewhere else. I never have any memories of what transpires."

"It was my husband, Mr. Slade. I'd know that voice anywhere. Isn't that right Gladys?" Mrs. DuVille asked.

"It certainly sounded like Herbert," that lady confirmed though her tone indicated that she didn't want to believe any of it.

"OK. It was your husband, Mrs. DuVille. Any idea what this item he wants me to pick up is?"

"No, I'm sorry I can't help you, Mr. Slade. All I know is that that barber shop is the one my husband had been going to for years."

"So, what now, Professor? Do we try to make contact again?"

"I doubt if that would be successful, Mr. Slade. These things take a great deal of effort on both sides. I take it though, that Mr. DuVille was able to get his message across to you"

"Yeah. If it isn't all a big joke being played on me."

"I'm afraid I don't understand," the Professor said. He genuinely appeared to be puzzled. Maybe he *hadn't* heard what was coming out of his mouth.

"I got the message, Professor. I'm just not sure it was worth the trouble."

"But you will go and fetch this package or whatever it is," Mrs. DuVille said with concern.

"It's what I'm getting paid for. I'll go tomorrow. If there's nothing else, I'll just be moseying along then. I'd like to thank you for an interesting evening, ladies."

"I'll be going, as well, Mrs. DuVille," the Professor informed her. "If you could call me a taxi?"

"I'd be glad to give you a ride, Professor," I said. There were still a few things that I wanted to discuss with the magician.

"I wouldn't want to put you to any trouble, Mr. Slade. A cab will be fine."

"Oh, it's no trouble at all. I'm probably going that way, anyhow."

"Thank you, then. You are a true gentleman." He didn't seem all that comfortable with accepting a lift, but he didn't see any way to refuse.

"Before you go, Professor," Mrs. DuVille said, handing him a small envelope. "And, thank you again. I have one for you as well, Mr. Slade."

I took the envelope and stuffed it in my jacket pocket. There didn't seem to be any need to check the contents.

My Chevy was still the only car parked out front besides Mrs. Johanssen's. It's not the newest heap, but it still runs. The professor didn't seem to bothered by this as he slipped into the passenger's seat. As a small time stage magician, I figured he'd probably ridden in a lot worse.

I got behind the wheel and started the engine. I was turning to ask the professor where he was headed when I noticed he was looking at me funny like I had a wart on my nose or something. He caught that I had noticed.

"I'm sorry, Mr. Slade. It's just that you have a most unusual aura."

"Aura?" I asked. I didn't have a clue what he meant. I wondered if it was just part of his magician act or if there was something more behind it.

"Every person, every living creature, even plants has a sort of glow surrounding them. Most people can't see it, but a few can. I am one of those few who is blessed, or cursed, with that ability. I've only seen an aura like yours around one other person, a singer that goes by the name Josephine LaTouche."

That gave me a start. I knew her, or him. She/he was a female impersonator and torch singer at a club called the Blue Angel. She was also one of the people tied into the whole Handler business. Of course the professor might have found this out and been trying to spook me, but there had been a look of uncertainty on his face as he examined my aura.

"So what does my aura tell you?"

"I haven't a clue, Mr. Slade. Not a clue."

I grunted at that and put the car into gear. "Where to, Professor?"

"The Blue Angel. It's a club on—"

"I know where it is," I interrupted, maybe more abruptly than was needed.

"I do a midnight show there, Tuesdays and Thursdays."

"I wouldn't think that magic tricks were their kind of thing." The Blue Angel attempted to recreate a Berlin cabaret from the period between the wars. Mostly it was just guys dressed up as girls, but a few of them, like LaTouche, had some real talent. I didn't necessarily see the appeal a stage magician would have for their usual audience.

" I think they find me amusing, camp I believe is the current word. Besides, I work cheap."

"Oh?"

"There really isn't that much call for stage magicians these days. I take what work I can get."

"Like Mrs. DuVille?" I asked with a disapproving tone.

"Like Mrs. DuVille," the professor replied. "I get the feeling you don't approve, Mr. Slade. Maybe you think I'm taking advantage of a poor widow. I assure you, I'm not. I'm just trying to make an honest buck. If you don't believe me, just look at the check."

He reached inside his jacket and pulled out the envelop Mrs. DuVille had given him. He jerked out the contents and waved it in front of my face. It was a picture of Grant on green paper. Fifty bucks. Not bad for less than an hour's work, but no fortune either. About what you'd expect to pay an entertainer for a kid's birthday party.

"Put your money away. You're distracting the driver."

He put the money away and sat in a silent huff. I was having a hard time figuring Longwell out. If he was some kind of huckster he either wasn't a very good one or he was so good at it that he could fool anyone. I couldn't decide which.

After a while I broke the silence with "So, how did you get into the séance racket, anyhow? You're seem a bright guy. I'd have thought you could do better."

"It's a long story, Slade."

"We've got time. It'll take twenty minutes at least to get to the Blue Angel."

He seemed to think that over for a bit, then started to unburden himself. It was like he had been dying to tell the story all his life.

"It started when I was a kid. Like a lot of kids back then I fooled around with magic tricks. You know, the kind of things you order out of the back of a comic book. Coin tricks, card tricks, that kind of thing. I wasn't any better than most kids at them. Except for the card tricks, that is. I was real good at guessing which card people picked. I always seemed to get it right. I was naïve enough not to know how strange that was. It wasn't till I ran into a carnie who was running a three card Monty stand with a circus that I discovered I had a talent. After I'd worked a quarter into a sawbuck guessing against him he closed the stand and took me aside. He tried a whole bunch of card tricks, hidden balls, all that kind of thing. I could guess them all. He had me run some tricks, too. Pick a card, any card, put it back in the pack. He couldn't fool me. He was real impressed. He said I should run away and join the circus and he would show me the ropes. Of course I didn't. I was twelve at the time. But a few years later, well, let's just say I didn't have any reason for sticking around anymore. The next carnival that came through town, I left with it.

"At first I was just a shill for a two-bit magician named 'El Magnifico,' then a warm up act, then an assistant. Within a year, 'El Magnifico' went off on a bender and I became the shows magician. I was lousy at first except for card tricks and mind reading shtick, but I learned quick. I wasn't making much money, magic acts aren't the big draw with a carnival, but I was eating regular which was more than a lot of folks were doing back then. Then the carnival went belly up someplace out in Kansas, for God's sake.

"I tried my hand at vaudeville, working my way around the country, improving my skills. Then that went bust, too. So now I do kiddy parties and drag bars and any other damned place that will pay me. So that's the story of my life."

I'd been listening with interest. It was quite a yarn. Half of it might even be true for all I knew.

"That doesn't explain the séance business," I observed.

"Well, living that life, you're always open for making a few bucks on the side. One of my best bits is the mind reading act. You know, take an article from someone in the audience and tell all about them, at least the stuff that won't get you into trouble. I got good at it. Some of the yokels started to think it was real. They wanted to have a private reading, get their fortune told, communicate with their late Aunt Fanny. That kind of thing. You can pick up a nice bit of change that way if you don't get greedy."

"And?"

The Professor hesitated for a moment. Like he wasn't sure if he wanted to go any farther down that road. Then he shrugged and went on. "Well, the fortune telling was no problem. You just tell 'em what they want to hear. The 'tall dark stranger,' they'd come into a small fortune, that kind of thing. You charge 'em a fin or a sawbuck, and get out of town and who'll ever care if it comes true or not."

"OK. I get that. But what about the talking with the dead?"

"That's where it gets a little strange, Slade. I thought I'd go in, do the fake trance, rattles on the knee bit. Make a few ambiguous statements in a falsetto and walk out with a few bucks. Like I said, I'm real good at reading people and telling them what they want to hear. I'd let them think they were communicating with their dearly departed and no real harm done.

"It doesn't always work out that way, though. I think it happened in Topeka the first time. Or maybe it was Wichita. I forget. I was doing a séance for a lady and her sister. She wanted to contact her husband who had recently passed away. I sat down at the table and was about to go into my fake trance. That's the last thing I remember. Next thing I know, the lights are back up and the lady is crying her eyes out and her sister is giving me dirty looks.

"I don't know what it was that I said while I was out. I never found out. But it turns out her husband wasn't all that unhappy with being dead. At least it got him away from his wife. I gather he wasn't too happy with being recalled, either. He evidently said 'the most awful things' to his wife.

"Well, if there is one thing a carnie learns, it's that the last thing a mark wants to hear is the truth. There's no money in it. And you never want to be out of control in a situation.

"I stopped doing séances for a while after that because, frankly, I was scared shitless. I didn't know if I was talking to the dead or going psychotic or what. But it was just too lucrative a sideline. I tried a few and didn't have any problems. Then one time in Rochester, up in Minnesota, it happened again. Except this time the departed and the living were still on speaking terms. After I came out of it one of the participants told me what had happened. They swore that it was the deceased speaking. It was his voice and he knew things that supposedly only he and his wife knew. They seemed happy enough. Gave me an extra twenty as a tip. I pocketed the money and ran. To this day, I don't have a clue as to what's going to happen."

I looked over at the Professor. In the light of the passing streetlights he looked almost relieved. Like he'd passed a kidney stone or something.

"So you're telling me this séance thing is legit? That it really is the dead speaking through your mouth? I find that a little hard to believe." Actually, given my recent past I was finding it a little *too* easy to believe.

"You can believe what you like, Slade. I don't know what to tell you. I'm never there when it happens, you understand. Maybe it's spirits, maybe it's just my subconscious, maybe it's the whole world playing a joke on me. I just don't know. All I can tell you is that I'm not faking it. You can believe that or not. Take your pick." Longwell seemed sincere. Of course he was a carnie.

"OK. So where does that leave me? What am I supposed to do?"

"As best I can figure, you should go to the barber shop and get the package. You might want to get a trim while you're at it, you're looking a little shaggy."

He was right about that. Janet had been nagging me about my hair all week.

By that time we were at the Blue Angel. I pulled into a spot by the curb so the Professor could get out.

"Thanks for the ride, Slade," the Professor said, leaning over the car after he had gotten out. "Say, I'm on in about fifteen minutes. Why don't you come on in and watch the show? I think you might enjoy it. I'll talk to the guy on the door and get him to skip the cover."

I thought about that. I needed some time to think. I could use a drink, too. "Why not?"

I followed the Professor down the steps leading to the door. A blast of loud music hit our ears as it opened, followed by a pair of drunks who stumbled up the steps. We entered and the Professor whispered something in the ear of the bouncer guarding the portal.

The Blue Angel is done up in what somebody thought a decadent '30s Berlin cabaret should look like. Somebody working on a small budget who had fallen asleep halfway through the movie. It had dim lights, small tables, and a lot of smoke. A bar ran along the wall on one side and a small stage occupied the far end of the main room. It's not exactly what they call a "gay" bar, but it's not known for being overly judgmental, either, as long as you didn't cause trouble.

The music died suddenly and the Professor said, "I've got to get ready for my show. You know where the bar is."

He was right about that. I knew the bartender slightly. At least he was the same one who had been tending bar the few times I'd been in. He nodded, came over, and took an order for a scotch and soda. I didn't want to get drunk. I just wanted to take the edge off.

On stage someone was picking up bits of clothing and setting up a few props. Suddenly a husky voice whispered in my ear, "Frankie, baby. Long time no see. What will Janet think?"

I turned around to face a buxom blonde, just under six feet, in a tight evening dress. It was Josephine LaTouche—also known as Joseph Jaworski during daylight hours—the headliner. She looked like the kind of broad they had used to adorn the noses of B-17s during World War II. That is if you didn't look too close. She could belt out a tune with the best of them and stayed in character better than most. She'd been an acquaintance of the late Ezekial O. Handler. Or had been a product of the same typewriter that had spawned me if you believed the writer's claims.

"Josephine," I said, saluting her with my glass. "Can I buy you a drink?"

"I thought you'd never ask, Frank," she said as she settled onto the barstool next to me. She waved a rather muscular arm clad in an elbow length opera glove at the bartender who responded with a nod.

"Slumming, Frank? You're a little late for the show. I just finished my last set."

"Actually, I'm here to see the Professor's act."

"I didn't know you were into magic."

"I'm not. But I was at a séance with the professor tonight and gave him a ride here."

"He's not half bad, Frank. Probably too good for this place. His mind-reading bit gives me the creeps, though. I'd watch that séance stuff, too."

At that point the stage lights dimmed for a moment and when they came up there was the Professor dressed in a rather ancient looking coat and tails. He bowed to the audience and began some shtick with pulling scarves out of his hand. He followed that by showing the audience the inside of his top hat. A few passes with a wand and he reached in and pulled a rather disturbed looking rabbit out of the hat. He set this onto the stage where it hopped around while the stage manager tried to catch it.

"Ladies and gentlemen," he announced, "of whichever gender." The latter got a rather stale laugh.

"I have here an ordinary deck of playing cards. Poker, not pinochle." About two people laughed at that one. "I'm going to ask one of you to pick a card from the deck and then replace it anywhere you like. I will then guess the card."

He handed the deck to a skinny guy at the nearest table. The geek fumbled with the deck and then picked a card and stuck it back in the deck.

"Now shuffle it, please."

The mark shuffled.

"Now hand it to your friend."

The mark handed it to the other person at the table. In the light I couldn't tell for sure what their sex was, though they were dressed in a skirt and sweater.

"The card was the seven of clubs," the Professor announced. He hadn't taken the deck back. There was a round of polite applause.

"Now, I will ask the young lady to think of a card." This seemed to take some effort on her part. "Do you have one in mind?" She nodded.

"The jack of diamonds."

She looked astounded. "Yes, that's what I was thinking of."

The Professor spent the next ten minutes with various card tricks and mind reading bits. He never tripped up. None of the tricks was particularly mind blowing; unless, that was, they weren't tricks.

About halfway through, Josephine slammed back what was left of her drink, stood up, and with a little wave of her glove clad fingers departed for the dressing room on her size fourteen heels.

When I looked back to the stage a long box on a stand had been wheeled up behind the Professor.

"And now, ladies and gentlemen, for my grand finale, I will saw a woman in half. If my lovely assistant will join me, please?"

His lovely assistant was the skinny guy in fishnet stockings and a poorly adjusted blonde wig who wandered around selling cigarettes. He made his way through the tables to the stage and with some aid on the Professor's part climbed awkwardly into the box.

The Professor closed the box so that his head and hands were poking out one end and his spike heel shod feet were out the other end. The professor removed one of these shoes and tickled the bottom of the protruding foot with a feather. The head at the other end withered in reaction.

"And now ladies and gentlemen, I will saw my assistant in half with this saw.'" He produced a big two handed logging saw from the back of the stage.

"If someone will assist me. Perhaps the gentleman drinking the scotch and soda at the bar. He looks like a strong able-bodied fellow." I looked around and realized he was talking to me. What the heck, I thought, and joined him on the stage.

"If you will check the saw, please?"

It felt like a real saw. I tested one of the teeth with the ball of my thumb. It was sharp.

"Can you verify that this is, in fact, a real saw."

"It feels like the real deal to me, but then I'm no lumberjack." That line got a bigger laugh than had any of the Professor's patter.

"If you will take up a position on that side of the box?" I was to the audience side with my back to them. The guy in the box wasn't looking too happy.

The Professor fitted the saw into a groove in the box. "Grab the handle. And pull."

We sawed away. It was quick work. About halfway through I thought I felt a bit of soft resistance. The guy in the box appeared to have fainted. We made it all the way through. I didn't see any blood dripping out on the stage.

The Professor did something with the box and the two halves separated rolling away on their stands. He took the saw and handed it to the stage manager and then thanked me and said I could sit down.

"I have now sawed my assistant in half. Thank you ladies and gentlemen, that concludes our show." And with that the Professor began to walk off the stage.

The stage manager came out to turn him around. I wasn't sure whether the look of horror on his face was part of the act or real.

The Professor turned to face the audience. "The stage manager seems to think the trick is unfinished. But ladies and gentlemen, I never promised to rejoin my assistant, did I?"

This got an uneasy laugh from the audience. The guy in the box still seemed to be passed out. The two parts of the box were separated by about three feet.

"Oh very well," the Professor said in a tone of fake exasperation.

He motioned to the stage manager to help him push the two parts of the box together. He latched them tight and then spun the box around several times until the head of the cigarette girl was pointing in the opposite direction from when they had started.

The Professor got a glass of water from a stand at the back of the stage and splashed it on the face of the guy in the box who sputtered to life, knocking his wig off.

"Are you alive?" the professor asked.

"I think so."

"Can you move your feet?"

The feet waggled up and down.

"That's a relief," the Professor said in mock tones.

"*You're* relieved—what about me?" the guy in the box asked in a squeaky voice.

The Professor bowed to the audience. "Thank you, ladies and gentlemen. That concludes the show. I will be back here every Tuesday and Thursday this month, so please tell all your friends."

I decided that I'd had enough of magic for one night and headed home.

My mind must have still been occupied with the magic act, because I was caught off guard when a big guy stepped out of the shadows and sucker punched me in the gut as I was fumbling for the keys of the Chevy. If I had been drinking more heavily that night I might have spilled my guts out on the sidewalk. As it was, I staggered back trying to catch my breath and waited for the follow up.

It never came. Instead, my assailant stepped back into the shadows just far enough so that I couldn't see his face. A second man stepped forward, though he too was careful to make sure his face was in the dark. The only part of him that I could see clearly was his feet. They were shod in expensive custom Italian shoes with a two buck shine.

"This is a warning Slade," a voice came out of the dark. It was a deep voice with just the hint of an Irish brogue. "Next time it won't be."

"Warning of what?" I asked, still breathless.

"To mind your own business and stay out of other people's. You were at the widow DuVille's tonight. If your game is to shake her down or play a con with that two-bit carney magician, forget it now. She's got friends."

"I'm not a grifter. I'm a P.I. It was her idea. She invited me to a séance. I only went because I thought someone might be taking advantage of her."

"Séance my eye, Slade. We both know there's no such things as ghosts. Drop the case or you might find that out personally."

I took that as a threat. I was about say something witty in protest when the fancy Italian shoes disappeared into the darkness. As I hobbled to my Chevy I wondered who the hell that had been and what I had gotten myself into. Mrs.

DuVille hadn't seemed the type to have Irish mobsters watching her back.

Janet was already asleep when I entered the apartment. It was amazing how short a time it had taken me to think of her place as "home." I still had kept my old place in the chauffeur's quarters above the garage of what had once been a mansion, but I was having trouble remembering the last time I had actually slept there. With someone like Janet as a drawing card, it was hard to see why I would.

I undressed in the bathroom. There was a little bruising where I had been hit, but nothing obvious. The guy that had hit me had been a pro. At least I didn't have any marks that I would have to explain to Janet. As quietly as I could I crawled into bed next to her. Somehow I managed to fall asleep without dreaming of dismembered transvestites or the Irish mob.

Janet let me sleep late. Another thing to recommend her, as if she needed it. While I was taking a shower, she was in the kitchen fixing eggs and bacon. It was times like that that made me think that maybe she really was the product of Handler's imagination. Looks and a good cook. What real woman could be so perfect?

Her timing was perfect, too, she was just placing my plate on the table when I entered the dining room. The coffee was already steaming in its cup. Janet, as usual, was forgoing a hearty breakfast and had a couple of pieces of fruit in front of her.

"You were out late, Frank," she said. It was a statement without reproach. "How was your séance?"

"It wasn't my séance. It was run by a guy goes by the name Professor Longwell. I had an interesting conversation with him afterwards."

"Oh?" she said.

"Yeah. He's a stage magician. Puts on a midnight show at the Blue Angel. That's where I was before I came home. I thought I'd catch the show."

"Was Josephine there?" Janet asked. There was a strange dynamic between those two that I don't pretend to understand. It's not like LaTouche is any sort of competition. It's not even like they are enemies. There's just a weird tension, kind of like the feeling you get right before a thunderstorm.

"I just missed her act. She stopped by for a drink and to say hello."

If there was a response to that, Janet buried it in a piece of melon.

Between mouthfuls of egg and bites of bacon I went on to recount the events of the night, ending it with a lurid description of the dismemberment of the cigarette "girl."

"It sounds gruesome," Janet commented, dabbing her lush lips with her napkin.

"You would have loved it," I said, not believing it for a moment. "I can't figure this Professor guy out. He acts like a two-bit stage magician, but there are times I think he might actually be the real deal.

"So, are you going to this barbershop?" Janet asked.

"Yeah. I don't see as how I've got any choice. Besides, you keep telling me I need a trim."

"Just be careful that he doesn't take too much off the top, Frank."

Al's Barbershop was in one of those older residential neighborhoods built when they still allowed small commercial buildings to occupy the corner lots. As I drove by looking for a parking spot I gave the place the once over. With the red and white striped pole beside the door and the gilt lettering on the plate glass window that made up the front of the shop it looked like it had probably been there for decades. It shared a building with another small shop that advertised that it repaired and sold clocks. I'm not the most up to date guy, but it was like stepping back in time a couple of decades.

A little bell rang as I walked in the front door. There were two chairs and one barber. I guessed that he was Al. He had the look of someone that had been cutting hair for thirty years. The guy in the chair was an old geezer. It had been at least that long since he had needed any "taken off the top."

I took a seat and picked up a copy of the "Police Gazette." It had been years since I had read one of those. I leafed through it, glancing at the stories of murder and mayhem. I gave a quick check of the date. The magazine was five years old. It didn't really matter. Crime is crime.

Al finished working on the old guy in the chair. The latter got up, paid his tab, said "same time next month?" and walked out without waiting for a reply. He probably didn't need to.

"Next," the barber said. I thought that was superfluous as I was the only other person in the joint.

"My girl friend says I need a trim job," I said as I climbed into the waiting chair.

"She's right," was Al's response as he draped the white cloth over me. It reminded me of an undertaker except he left my head sticking out.

Al made with the scissors. He wasn't much of one for small talk, it seemed. There was an old radio on the long counter that ran under the mirror that ran the length of the wall the shop shared with the clock place, but it wasn't on. I had a feeling it was only turned on when there was a ball game.

Al appeared to know his business. It was less than ten minutes before he spun the chair around so I could see myself in the big mirror. He hadn't done too bad a job. A little out of style, but then so was I. He made with the little brush, slapped some scented stuff on my neck, and said, "That'll be three dollars."

I got out my wallet, handed him four and said, "I believe a friend of mine left something for me. I was told to say that Ray Nitschke sent me."

"Was that Ray Nitschke the football player?" he asked suspiciously.

"No. It was Ray Nitschke the German philosopher."

That answer seemed to satisfy Al. "That Herb was always a great kidder."

I wasn't prepared to believe that, but maybe to Al he was.

"I've got it right here, somewhere," he said. He rummaged around amongst the drawers and cubby holes in the counter and finally came up with an envelope. It was a regular letter sized envelope. White. As Al handed it to me I noted that it had written on the front "From Ray."

"Did you know Herb long?" I asked.

"Over twenty years. Came in regular. Every three weeks whether he needed it or not. Thursdays. 9:30." That seemed to be the sum of Al's knowledge of the late Mr. DuVille. Didn't seem like much for twenty years.

"Did you want to make another appointment?"

I looked at myself in the mirror. "I'll think about it. See what my girlfriend thinks."

The bell above the door rang as I left.

I waited until I was back in my car before I opened the envelope. What I found inside was a key. No paper, no explanation, just a key. The question was, what did it unlock?

I drove back to the office. Once there I sat behind my desk, put the key in front of me and looked at it. It was an ordinary enough key, about two inches long. It looked like it might open a locker someplace, the question was where. There wasn't anything on it to indicate what it was the key to. The only writing on it was the legend "Do Not Duplicate" stamped into the handle and a five digit number.

I was still staring at it when there was a knock at the door. I went to see who it was. The knocker was a short, slim man who looked to be in his late forties. He was wearing a good quality suit that was neither flashy or new. It wasn't off the rack because it had been tailored to his build by someone who knew his business. He had dark hair that was starting to thin where it was combed back from his forehead. He carried a big briefcase in his left hand, one of those with the sloping sides, sturdy but well worn.

"Mr. Slade?" he asked in a tone that didn't sound like he was a salesman.

"That's me," I replied.

"My name is Abe Silver," he said handing me a business card. I didn't think that he was named after the president from Illinois. The card said "Abraham Silver, Mid-Continental Insurance Company" and listed a P.O. Box address and a phone number. I knew of Mid-Continental by reputation, which was that they were honest but also diligent. They handled mostly commercial insurance for businesses though they also did the occasional life insurance policy for executives.

"Come in, Mr. Silver. Have a seat."

He entered the office, taking it in in an appraising once over that neither indicated approval or disapproval. He sat down, placing the briefcase on the floor next to him.

"What can I do for you, Mr. Silver?" I said when I was back in my desk chair.

"I understand that you are working for Mrs. Herbert DuVille. Is that correct?"

"Why the interest, Mr. Silver, if you don't mind my asking?"

"My company carried a policy on Mr. DuVille. A rather substantial policy for five hundred thousand dollars, twice that in the event of an accident. It was taken out a few months before his death. It is company policy in cases where death occurs so soon after a policy was taken out to investigate the circumstances."

"I would hate to do anything that would cause Mrs. DuVille problems in collecting," I said noncommittally.

"You misunderstand me, Mr. Slade. Mrs. DuVille isn't the beneficiary. Her husband had a policy with another company, one that he had taken out some years ago for which she was the beneficiary. She has already collected on that, I believe. The policy in question was taken out by his partners, a Mr. McClure and a Mr. Trentino."

"Interesting," I said.

"Such policies are not that unusual in partnerships you understand, and it may be just a coincidence that Mr. DuVille met his demise so soon after the policy was taken out, but prudence dictates that we verify the facts in the case."

"You're an investigator for the insurance company, Mr. Silver?"

"Oh, no, Mr. Slade. I'm not a detective like yourself. I'm just a guy who goes around and asks the questions that need to be asked until I get the answers that are needed."

It sounded like the same thing to me. I was getting the impression that Abe Silver was pretty good at getting answers to his questions.

"That sounds reasonable. How can I help you, Mr. Silver?"

"Please call me Abe, Mr. Slade." Now that it appeared I was willing to cooperate, it seemed Silver was willing to drop the formality. Just two professionals going about their business.

"I'm Frank," I replied. I was willing to go along. I had nothing against Mid-Continental, and it didn't seem that they had any interest in doing anything against my client.

"Getting back to my original question, Frank, are you working for Mrs. DuVille?"

"She asked me to a séance."

"A séance?" he asked skeptically.

"That's what I thought, Abe. I really only agreed because I thought some con-man might be trying to take advantage of her. But it seemed more or less legit."

"I guess I'm a little surprised. That wasn't what I expected. So she hasn't asked you to investigate her husband's death?"

"No, just the séance and run a little errand for her. I'm a little behind things. Abe. Just how did Mr. DuVille meet his death?"

"It appears to have been an accident. He was crushed by a falling crate at the warehouse associated with his trucking company."

"Nothing suspicious about it?"

"Not on the surface. No one else was in the warehouse at the time and there were no indications of foul play. Still, it does seem a coincidence coming so soon after the policy was taken out, and insurance companies really don't like coincidences."

"Not at a million bucks."

"Precisely, Frank."

"Anything else besides it just being a coincidence?"

"Curiously it turns out that something similar happened a few years ago in Moline. The active partner in a business that Mr. McClure had invested in died in a car accident. There was nothing suspicious at the time, but McClure did collect on a hundred thousand dollar policy. Something of a coincidence, don't you think, Frank?"

"And you don't like coincidences."

"No, I guess I don't."

"I wish I could help you out, Abe, but it's like this. I just started working for Mrs. DuVille yesterday, and like I said, she just wanted me to take part in a séance. She said that her husband had something to tell me."

"And did he?"

"That's the funny thing, Abe. He did. He wanted me to pick up this key here," I said pointing to the key laying on the desk blotter. "The thing is, I haven't got a clue as to what it unlocks."

Silver took a careful look at the key.

"I think I might be able to help you there, Frank. It's the key to a Post Office Box. The East Side Branch, if I'm not mistaken."

"How'd you know that, Abe?" I said raising my eyebrows.

"I happen to have one just like it. For the P.O. Box on my card. I'm pretty sure it's for the East Side office because they use a different style downtown." As if to prove his point he reached inside his pants pocket and produced a key ring. On it was a key identical to mine except for the serial number stamped into the handle.

"That's quite a coincidence," I said. Abe just shrugged.

"Any idea what box number?"

"I'm afraid I can't help you there Frank. The ID number on the key has nothing to do with the box. They do that so that if the key is lost someone can't use it. You'd have to check with the Postmaster, but they don't like to give that information out without a good reason.

"Too bad. But at least that's something. Maybe I can find out which box it's for some other way."

"I'm sure you can, Frank. After all, you *are* a detective," Abe said with a smile. I thought to myself that I could get to like this guy. Or hate him.

"Anything else I can do for you, Abe?"

"There is one other thing. You've heard about the jewelry store robbery? The one where the two people were killed?"

"Only what I've read in the papers. Any connection?"

"I don't think so. It's just that my company carried a policy on the store. A fairly substantial one. Over a million. Mid-Continental will be quite generous with anyone who comes forward with information leading to the recovery of what was taken. If you hear of anything let me know."

"I'll keep that in mind, Abe. Kind of a coincidence, though, isn't it?"

"What do you mean, Frank?"

"Mid-Continental having to make two big payouts for things that happened within a few days of each other."

"I never thought about it before. It is a coincidence," he said thoughtfully.

"And you don't like coincidences, do you? I'll get in touch, Abe, if I hear anything."

"Thanks, Frank. I'll be going now. I can let myself out." He picked up his briefcase and left.

After he left, I stared at the key again. A Post Office Box. It made sense in a way, if you wanted to keep something safe. More anonymous than a deposit box at a bank, nearly as safe, and easier to access if you had the key and knew the box number. You could put something in it just by stuffing it in an envelope and dropping it in a mailbox. No one would suspect anything. It left me with a lot of questions. What Herbert had stashed away in his box? What was worth coming back from the dead to tell me about? And, if anyone else knew about the key?

I clipped the key onto my key-chain. As an afterthought, I rummaged around the center drawer of my desk. There'd been a key there when I'd moved in. I'd never figured what lock it went to, but I'd never tossed it out, either. It was about the right size. I found it next to the paperclips. I dropped the key into the envelope I'd gotten at the barbershop and put it in the top drawer on the right under a copy of the city directory. Not really hidden, but not in plain sight, either.

By that time it was noon and despite breakfast I was feeling hungry. I locked the office door behind me and headed to a bar down the street that served a decent burger.

It's getting harder for a tavern to get by these days just selling booze and beer. The down side is that some great old drinking establishments have closed. The upside is that it's become easier to get a decent sandwich and a cold one as the clever owners have added grills and are offering more than peanuts and pickled eggs to their patrons.

Unfortunately, I'd hit the place at the peak of the noon rush and there weren't any open seats at the bar. Luckily I spotted Lt. Flannigan sitting at a table.

"Mind if I join you, Flannigan? The barstools are full."

"Something you want to talk to me about, Frank?" Flannigan asked suspiciously. The lieutenant and I aren't quite what you'd call friends. Not quite enemies, either.

"No. It's just that I'm hungry and I don't want to wait around for a seat."

"Suit yourself," Flannigan said, taking another bite out of his corned-beef on rye.

I caught the eye of the waitress and ordered a burger and fries with a slice of raw onion and a tap beer.

"Janet's going to love that. I don't see what she sees in you, Slade."

"My innate charm, I guess. You seem your usual grumpy self."

"It's this jewelry robbery case they got me on. A bad business, and not much in the way of clues."

"That the one where two people were killed?"

"Yeah. The owner and his bookkeeper. From what everyone says she was a nice lady that had been working there for twenty years."

"They didn't print much in the way of details in the paper."

"The two of them, the owner, Benjamin Silver, and his bookkeeper, Susan Fishbein, were doing an inventory. It was after hours and the lights in the front of the store were off. The burglars broke in, were surprised by the owner, and shot the two of them. No one heard the shots, but that's not surprising. The places on either side were closed for the night and the floor above is used as storage space. The murders were done with a small caliber gun, probably an automatic. Maybe even with a silencer. The crooks were probably pros. They came in through the back door. Punched out the lock with a sledge hammer. The alarm wasn't on, because the owner was still there. No prints, no witnesses. They took about a million and a quarter of ice, left the watches and junk. We figure there were two of them, but that's just a guess. Probably from out of town. All the local talent either has alibis or are in the lockup. Why the interest?"

"Curiosity. I was just talking to an insurance guy from Mid-Continental about it."

"Abe Silver?"

"Yeah. Any relation to the owner?"

"He didn't mention it. I thought you were getting out of the shamus racket, Frank."

"I am. He came into my office on an unrelated matter."

Flannigan grunted. "How'd your séance go? Longwell trying to con the old lady?"

"Not as far as I could tell. He seems legit, or at least as legit as a magician can be. If he's conning the DuVille broad for money, it's chump change. He showed me a check for fifty bucks. She paid me twice that for showing up."

"Maybe you're the one I should run in for conning a widow."

"I haven't cashed the check yet. Besides, I'm doing some leg work for her."

"I didn't think you went in for that kind of thing, Frank," Flannigan said with a leer.

"Keep your mind out of the gutter, Flannigan. It seems her old man left something behind she wants me to collect. I'm trying to find it."

"What?"

"I don't know yet. I found out about it during the séance."

"Who told you?"

"Her husband."

"Oh. Hey, wait a minute isn't he dead—?" Flannigan sputtered.

"Yeah. Screwy, isn't it?"

The waitress dropped off my burger and Flannigan's check.

"I've got to go do some honest work, Frank. Not like some of us. Enjoy the burger." Flannigan stood up, stuck his hat back on his head and left. I was halfway through the burger when I noticed he'd left me to pay his bill.

I got back to the office about one. As I reached up to stick the key in the lock I noticed something. There were some slight scratching by the key slot barely visible in the dim light of the corridor. I didn't think they had been there when I'd locked up before lunch. I could just see them, but the bottoms of the scratches were bright unlike the dull brass of the rest of the lock face.

I entered the office cautiously, but it was empty. It hadn't been ransacked either, at least so I could notice. But then things hadn't been all that neat, either. The file cabinets were still locked, but if someone had picked the deadbolt lock on the door, the cabinets would have been child's play.

I opened the drawer where I'd put the key. The directory was still in place, but when I lifted it, the envelope was gone. I rummaged around the drawer to see if it had been pushed out of place, but no luck. Just to make sure, I checked the other drawers, as well. Nothing else was missing, but the envelope with the key was still gone.

I sat down in my desk chair and stared at the door. The lock on the door was a deadbolt, not the kind of thing you can get past with a credit card. There hadn't been any jimmy marks around the frame. Now a lock like that isn't that hard to pick with the right tools and experience. I knew probably a couple of dozen guys who could do it, at least half of whom were not in prison at the moment. But it was looking like the work of a pro, not an amateur. They had known what they were after and hadn't left a mess, either.

For a moment I thought about calling in the cops, but only for a moment. I'd look the fool, and there wouldn't be much they could do. There wouldn't be any prints and the only thing that had been stolen was a worthless key. The report would be filed away and forgotten.

There was only one thing to do. That was make a visit to the post office.

The East Side Post Office isn't a fancy Beaux Arts building like the one downtown, with pillars and wide granite steps confirming the power and the might of the federal government. It's in a plain brick building from the 60's on a side street. It shares a parking lot with a Laundromat and a tax accountant. It's meant to be a convenient place for local businesses to collect and send their mail and for people in the neighborhood to drop off packages at Christmas.

Like hundreds of other branch post offices it has a glass door leading into a counter area. Posters of stamps and examples of mailing envelopes line the walls of the small foyer fronting the counter. There are a couple of stamp machines off to the side. You can post mail by sticking the envelopes through a set of slots next to the counter, one for local, one for non-local, one for air-mail and foreign. You get the feeling that behind the wall, they all drop the letters into the same bin.

Around the corner is the area for post-office boxes, conveniently located just out of the view of the clerk at the counter. I wandered nonchalantly around that corner. It was the middle of the afternoon and the east side branch is a small office. No one was there to observe me.

I had the key. The question was, which box had belonged to DuVille. There were only a hundred or so boxes, stacked ten to a column. A few larger sized boxes were off to the side. I could try all of them until I found one that the key fit, but even in a slow branch like that, I'd probably attract attention before I found the right box.

Then it struck me. DuVille had been a sharp guy in his own way. He had wanted me to be able to find the right box, hadn't he? Otherwise, why contact me from beyond the grave? So what clue had he given me. He'd said to tell Al the barber that Ray Nitschke had sent me? That had seemed pointless and rather silly at the time. But was it? Nitschke had been a football player. He'd worn a number, 66. The small sized boxes were numbered 000 to 099.

I took out my keychain and stuck the key into the lock of 066. It fit the slot, and when I gave it a twist, it turned, popping the door open. I looked inside the little cubbyhole. Sure enough, there was a fat, legal sized envelope waiting inside. I pulled it out, stuck it in my jacket pocket and closed the door of the box back up and walked out of the post office like it was something I did every day.

The clerk behind the counter saw me as I exited. She waved and said, "Bye." You got to love the Post Office.

I drove a couple of blocks, just far enough to make sure I wasn't being tailed, then pulled over and parked. Was I being melodramatic? It isn't everyday you get sent on a treasure hunt by a ghost. But was it all just an elaborate practical joke? Only one way to find out.

I pulled out the envelope and looked at the front. It was addressed to Herbert DuVille, P.O. Box 66. There was no return address. There were two first class stamps in the upper right hand corner. The envelope was heavy, and DuVille had wanted to make sure that it wasn't discarded for insufficient postage. The post mark was local, the date was the day that DuVille had had his accident with a 6:00 PM time stamp. DuVille had stuffed it in a mailbox for the evening pickup and then gone to his fatal encounter with a packing crate.

I pulled out my pocketknife and slit the top of the envelope. Inside were about a dozen sheets of typewritten paper, the first of which was a cover letter of sorts.

"To Whom It May Concern

I must assume that if you are reading this, I am dead. I have no way of knowing just how or when this letter will fall into your hands. The post office box to which this was posted is one that I took out just a few weeks ago, and no one knows of its existence. The key I have placed with a trusted friend to whom I have given a password of sorts. He has no idea what the key is to, or about the contents of this letter.

I also have no way of knowing how or when I may have died, but I have my suspicions that it will not have been of natural causes or due to an accident, whatever the appearances may be. I also assume that my demise will have occurred shortly after this letter was posted.

Some time ago, I took on several partners to my business in order to obtain funds for expansion. They came highly recommended and the agreement was that they would take little of an active role in the business. I have since discovered, however, that these two men are not honest businessmen, but instead have been using my business as a 'front' for various illegal purposes. I have detailed my evidence for this belief in the enclosed attachments.

What I ask is that whoever recovers this letter turn the information over to the appropriate authorities. However, I must caution you to be careful because these men are extremely dangerous and have been responsible for the deaths of at least several people.

I also ask that you convey my regrets and love to my wife of thirty years at such a time as you may safely do this. I only wish that I had not let my ambitions get the better of me.

Herbert C. DuVille"

The language was a little stilted, but I had to admire DuVille, both for his courage and for the ingenuity he had used to protect the information. I had to wonder, though, had he really spoken from the spirit world, or had he at some point taken Professor Longwell into his confidence.

I glanced through the attached sheets. It appeared that McClure and Trentino had been operating as large scale fences using the facilities of the trucking company as a cover. They would collect stolen goods, mostly high value items like electronics, auto parts, and other bulky items, and ship them to distant cities where they could be sold without attracting the attentions of the local police. They were also shipping in goods that had been stolen in other cities and selling them locally as legitimate items. As a legitimate trucking company, a few extra cartons of merchandise off the record would never be noticed. Deliveries could be made directly to the final customer without drawing attention. And with the company's warehouse space, stolen goods could sit for months until the heat on them had died down. The operation seemed to have covered at least a three state area. As a plan it was almost brilliant in its conception.

DuVille had uncovered one of the shipments by accident, but once he became aware, he had noted and recorded every illegal shipment that he discovered. He had listed over a hundred such shipments.

It was the last page that really caught my interest, though. Not content just to act as fences, McClure and Trentino were using the trucks to move professional thieves around without attracting attention. Out of town talent would be brought in as assistant drivers, pull off a job, and then slip away on another truck along with their loot.

Of course, that would only pay off if the crooks were part of the criminal elite, like experienced safe-crackers or burglars. It wouldn't pay for two-bit punks who were more muscle than brain.

I thought about the crew that had knocked over the jewelry store. Flannigan had said that he didn't think it had been done by any of the local crooks. Could they have been brought in by McClure and Trentino?

I stuffed the sheets back into the envelope. Obviously, the information was dynamite. But would anyone believe me? After all, though DuVille had gone into great detail, the information wasn't proof, it was hearsay. And the fact that they'd been passed to me by a dead guy didn't help.

The big question was what to do with the envelope? My office had already been broken into, and I couldn't see the tin can of a safe that I had being any hindrance to McClure and Trentino, particularly as they seemed to have a talented safecracker on their team. My apartment wasn't any better a choice. And I didn't want to drag Janet into this if I could help it.

I leaned back in the seat of my car trying to think. Then I looked up and it struck me. Down on the corner was a drugstore. A sign in the window advertised copies for a quarter. I didn't bother to lock the car when I got out. I'd probably be better off if someone stole the heap.

Inside the drugstore I found the copier. It was coin operated. I went to the checkout counter and bought a roll of quarters. A few minutes later, I had two sets of copies. A trip to the stationary aisle and I had three manila envelopes. I stuffed the originals into one of them and the copies into the other. The clerk at the counter was real helpful. She lent me a pen to address two of them. The one with the originals I sent right back to DuVille's P.O. box. I figured it had worked once, it should work again. The second set I addressed to my office. The third set I kept with me. The clerk even had a postage scale to weigh them so I could get the correct number of stamps. She pointed to the mailbox on the corner. I gave her a cheery good bye, dropped the two envelopes into the box and returned to my car.

It was still there. Either I was in a respectable neighborhood, or the local car thieves were too picky to nab an old Chevy.

It was getting close to four in the afternoon when I pulled away from the curb. I should still have time to catch Flannigan. I headed downtown to the police headquarters.

The sergeant on the front desk didn't know me from Adam, but a call up to Flannigan got me a visitor's badge.

"This had better be good, Frank," the lieutenant growled as I reached his desk. "I'm up to my ears in the jewelry store murders, and I haven't got a clue to work on."

"Maybe this will help," I replied, dropping the envelope on his desk.

He opened it, spread the sheets out on his desk giving them a quick once over.

"Is this some kind of joke, Frank? If it is, it ain't funny."

"It's legit, Flannigan."

"How'd you come by this stuff? And why hasn't it surfaced before?"

"DuVille must have suspected he was in danger. He put his notes in an envelope and mailed them to a P. O. box no one knew he had. It's been sitting there nice and safe protected by the full power of the U.S. government until I retrieved it this afternoon."

"How'd you find out about the box? And how'd you get the key? Intercepting the mail is a federal offence, Frank."

"You wouldn't believe me if I told you."

"This info won't do me any good unless I know it's legit. Spill the story, Frank, or leave me alone."

I went into the whole tale, from the séance to the barbershop to Abe Silver cluing me into the fact that the key was to a P.O. box.

"You expect me to believe that fairy tale?"

"I swear it's true, Flannigan. Every word."

"You expect me to believe that this DuVille character came back as a ghost—"

"Spirit."

"Whatever, and dropped word during a séance about a key to a secret mailbox where he wrote down everything that the McClure and Trentino and their gang were doing? I can't go to the D.A. with a story about spooks and spirits and things that go bump in the night."

"Look. I know it sounds screwy. I don't believe in the supernatural any more than you do. For all I know, DuVille knew Professor Longwell, and the whole séance rigmarole is just a con the two of them worked out to protect Mrs. DuVille."

"You really think that, Frank?"

"It makes as much sense as anything else, doesn't it? And at least it's something you might be able to sell the D.A."

"You're right about that, at least. So, what did you do with the original?"

"I wasn't sure I could protect them. My office has already been burgled. So I stuck them in another envelope and mailed it to DuVille's P.O. box. I used your name for the return address."

"Thanks a heap, Frank," Flannigan said wiping his beefy hands over his face. "Maybe that was the smart thing to do, after all. At least they're safe for awhile. Can I keep the copy?"

"Sure. I made another copy and mailed it to my office."

"Cute, Frank. But you'd better hope not too cute."

"So what do we do now?" I asked.

"What do you mean do?"

"With the info."

"*We* do nothing, Frank. All I've got are some dates and addresses. *I* will check them out against stolen property reports and see if there are any matches. If they check out, then *I* go present the information to the D.A. and try to gloss over how I came by the dope."

"What do you want me to do?"

"You're awfully slow on the uptake, Frank. You do nothing. This is official police business now, and I don't need some private shamus gumming up the works. Go home. Have dinner with Janet, though what she sees in you I'll never understand. Just let the police do their job. Got it, Frank?"

I gave him a hurt puppy expression. "If that's the way you want to play it, Flannigan."

"That's the way we're going to play it. I'll let you know if I need you. Now go home! And Frank, be careful. We know these guys play rough."

At dinner, Janet asked how my day had gone. I recounted my adventure with Al the barber and my visit to the post office. She said the haircut looked nice. Sometimes she doesn't quite seem real. She's got plenty on the ball when she needs it, but she can act the dumb blonde to perfection. Maybe that had been the appeal she had had for Handler, as if she had needed one beyond the long legs and sweet curves.

She looked down at the chicken on her plate pensively, then asked, "Do you believe in ghosts, Frank?"

"Ghosts? Not really. Why?"

"But the séance? The voice that led you to the key and the post office box? How else can you explain it?"

"I can't, honey. Not really. Maybe DuVille let this Longwell guy in on what he suspected. The Professor might just be trying to get the information to the cops without being too involved personally."

"Don't you think there's got to be more to it, than that, Frank?"

I could see that it was really bothering her. I'd never showed her the final letter that Handler had written to me, the one where he claimed that Janet, Flannigan, LaTouche and myself were just products of his imagination and some spell he had found in an old book. But she had been around all during the investigation and had seen the notes Handler had left before he was killed, the ones that seemed to predict what we were doing every step of the way until the moment Janet had saved my life by shooting the murderer. Even if she wasn't sure, she had to suspect that there was something decidedly odd about our lives.

"I'm not sure I do, Janet. I'm not sure that it matters. All I know is that I came up with the key and that led to the papers and I've turned it all over to Flannigan. It's his problem now."

"So you're going to drop it?"

"Flannigan made it pretty clear that that's what he wants me to do."

"But is that right?"

"You were the one who said she wanted me out of the detective business."

"I know I said that, and I meant it, but don't you have a duty to your client, Frank?"

I could see where this was leading to, and the truth was, I pretty much agreed with her.

"My client is Mrs. DuVille, not her dead husband. I'll keep an eye on things to make sure nothing happens to her. I'll help Flannigan, too, if he asks me. As to the ghost business, let's just say I'll keep an open mind for the time being."

"I know you'll do the right thing, Frank. Are you ready for dessert?"

I was hanging around my office the next day when Professor Longwell popped in. He seemed to have a bee under his bonnet.

"What's the idea, Slade?"

"Idea about what?"

"Setting the cops on me, that's what."

"I don't know what you're talking about."

"Some flat-footed lieutenant named Flannigan came poking around asking questions. Questions about me. I don't know nothing."

"Flannigan's okay. Besides, he's homicide, not bunko, and he's got a lot more on his plate than some magician who saws fake women in half and has a sideline as a card reader. At least as long as you manage to put whoever you saw in half back together again."

"Oh that. The saw bit. That's just a trick and an old one, at that. Kenny, that's the cigarette girl, folds himself up into half the box. The feet are fakes."

"I'm glad to hear that. I wouldn't want to hear that you'd killed Kenny,"

"No chance, shamus."

"Is that all you came for, to vent about the cops?"

"No. I wanted to warn you. Some big Irish tough, name of McClure, tried to put the fear of God into me last night. Said I should lay off Mrs. DuVille. I figured he might try the same with you."

"You're too late by a day and a half, Professor," I responded. "So that's McClure."

"Whose McClure?" the Professor asked, puzzled at the direction the conversation had veered.

"McClure was one of Herbert DuVille's partners. The ones who got his company when he died. And who stand to collect on a great big insurance policy to boot."

"Well I wouldn't trust him. I think he's a crook. How'd the treasure hunt go?"

"It went swell. There was a package. It had a key. That led to another package and that's where it got interesting. The late Herbert DuVille left some dirt about what his partners had been doing. That's why Flanigan came nosing around. I suspect he wants to know how you knew about the key."

"But I didn't. I swear. I was blanked out during the whole séance. I didn't know anything about the barbershop until you told me afterwards."

"I'm not sure Flannigan will buy that. He's looking for a better witness than a dead guy and he was hoping you were it."

"Not me. That reminds me. I was at another séance at Mrs. DuVille's last night. Herbert left a message. He wants you, this Lt. Flannigan, and some guy named Abe Silver to be present at another séance tomorrow. He said it was important. You know who this Silver guy is?"

"I know him. He's an insurance investigator. I can get in touch with him. I'm not sure he'll come, though."

"Hey, I just pass on the messages," the Professor protested.

"I'll see if I can arrange things."

"Good, because I'm not sure how much longer the connection with Herbert is going to hold. Last night was a real struggle and he only had time to pass on his message before he faded. At least that's what they told me. I've got to get going, the rabbit has got an appointment with the vet."

Flannigan's city issued sedan was already there when I pulled up in front of the DuVille house. There was another car as well, a two year old black and gold Pontiac. I figured that it belonged to Abe Silver. It looked like the kind of car he'd drive, big and comfortable but not as flashy as a Cadillac.

Esmeralda met me at the door as before, taking my hat and ushering me into the same room as my previous visit. The same table was set up in the middle of the room. I noticed that there were still only four chairs around it. Flannigan and Silver were standing around awkwardly, but Professor Longwell hadn't showed up yet. Mrs. DuVille was trying to make polite conversation, but not succeeding.

"This better be worth my time, Slade," Flannigan said as I entered the room.

"It was the last time," I replied. Flannigan huffed at that, but made no further comment.

"I must admit that I'm a little confused about what this is all about, Frank," Abe Silver chimed in. "You said that you had additional information about the jewelry store robbery."

"Not me, Abe. Mr. DuVille is the one with the information."

"But he's dead, isn't he?"

"He's dead, alright, but Professor Longwell seems to be able to communicate with him. What we're here for is in the way of a séance."

"A séance, Mr. Slade?"

"Yeah. Sitting around in the dark holding hands and speaking with dead people. I know it sounds goofy, but the last time I was here it led me to the lowdown on McClure's and Trentino's operation. Tonight I hope he delivers an even bigger bombshell."

"I don't know what to think. My religion doesn't really recognize such things. But I guess that if there is the possibility of obtaining information that would be beneficial to my company I can see it through."

"I was hoping you'd see it that way. I take it we're still waiting on the Professor?" I asked.

"I'm sure he will be here shortly, gentlemen," Mrs. DuVille assured us. "I've always found him to be punctual."

Again, as if on cue, the front doorbell rang. Maybe the Professor's psychic powers included timing his entrances perfectly. A few moments later Esmeralda led the Professor in. I made the introductions.

"If we're ready?" the Professor asked without preamble. "Good, then if you will take your seats, gentlemen. Frank, you can sit where you did before. The lieutenant should sit on your right and Mr. Silver to your left."

"What about Mrs. DuVille?" I asked.

"Mr. DuVille was clear in his instruction. It is to be just the four of us. I'm sorry, Mrs. DuVille."

"Oh, no, Professor. I understand completely. Herbert never did want me involved in his business. I'll leave you gentlemen to it then."

We took our allotted seats. Mrs. DuVille dimmed the lights on the way out and shut the French doors leading to the hall.

The procedure was the same as before. We each took the hands of the persons sitting next to us forming a ring. For a few minutes nothing happened, then there was the same flickering of the candles on the mantle and a sudden chill in the room. There was enough light for me to see the Professor, but as far as I could tell he had remained motionless in a trance.

"I must be brief," came out of the Professor's mouth, but in the same voice as during the previous séance, but this time it sounded weaker and farther off. "It becomes more difficult for me to make contact."

"Go ahead, Mr. DuVille, we're ready" I said.

"In the warehouse, on the southwest corner, there is a carton. It is marked 'X-300 Stereo Receiver' and it has a shipping label indicating the destination as Dubuque. Inside the box is the merchandise stolen from the jewelry store. It is set to be shipped in two days."

"So McClure and Trentino *were* behind the robbery," Flannigan exclaimed.

"Who were the robbers?" I asked.

"I don't know," came the voice, fainter than at first. "All I know is that they were from Peoria."

"Is there anything else you can tell us?" There was silence.

"Herbert, your death wasn't an accident, was it?" I hazarded.

"No!" The voice was almost a whisper.

"Who did it?" There was no reply. I asked several more times, but there was only silence.

We sat there in the darkness for five minutes or more, but nothing happen. No candle flickers, no temperature drops, only dead air. Finally the Professor came out of his trance. I got up and turned on the lights.

"Well, Flannigan. What do you say now?"

"What am I supposed to say, Frank?"

"You can pin the jewelry store robbery on McClure and Trentino."

"How? Just because this carney, no offense Longwell, claims the loot is in a box in the warehouse doesn't mean I can do anything about. Even if it's true and the ice is there, how can I prove it. Am I supposed to go to the D.A. and have him get a search warrant? Based on what? A séance? Come off it, Frank. I'd be laughed out of court. I'd be lucky to keep my badge. Hell, they'd probably lock me up in the loony bin. I can't say that I'd blame them, either."

"Can't you claim an anonymous tip or something?" I protested.

"It won't wash. Even if I did try to fudge it, it would never hold up. Word of this party tonight would get out and even if I did get a warrant, the evidence would probably be thrown out because it was improperly obtained. And that's even if I did believe this story, which I'm not sure I do."

I glared at him, trying to think of something to say, but I knew he was right. Flannigan wasn't happy, either. He'd love nothing better than to come down on McClure and Trentino, but he knew he didn't have any grounds to go on.

"Gentlemen, if I may make a suggestion." It was Abe Silver. So far he'd remained silent since the séance, but now he spoke up.

"My company still has an outstanding claim for Mr. DuVille's death. A one million dollar claim, I might add because of the double indemnity clause in case of an accident. Because that claim has been made, I am authorized to make an examination of the site of the accident. If they deny me access, the company can refuse to pay. They might even be able to threaten a lawsuit based on a fraudulent claim."

"Yeah, that sounds promising. What are you proposing?"

"That I go in and while I'm investigating the 'accident' I look for this carton. If I find it and open it and the jewelry is there, that gives probable cause. I'm sure that the lieutenant can take it from there."

"You know it could be dangerous, Silver," Flannigan said. "It already looks like they may have knocked off DuVille. That is if we can believe his ghost."

"I realize that, lieutenant. But not only is my company on the line for over two million between the robbery and the policy on Mr. DuVille, but the owner of the store was a relative. True, only a second cousin that I barely knew, but still, blood. I want justice for him. That's why I suggest that Mr. Slade comes with me. That should offer enough protection, don't you think?"

"It's your neck, Silver," Flannigan said. Somehow he forgot to mention mine.

"When are we going to do this? It sounds like they're planning on moving the goods in a couple of days."

"I would suggest as soon as possible," Silver answered. "Tomorrow morning. The two of us go in. The lieutenant and a few of his men can be waiting outside if we find anything."

"It sounds like a plan to me," Flannigan agreed.

"I'll meet you at your office tomorrow morning, then, Frank," Silver said as he stood up to go.

"OK by me. Say eight?"

"Fine. It's been an interesting evening, hasn't it?"

"I'd better go, too," Flannigan said. "I'll have to convince the captain, and that may not be easy."

"If things are breaking up, could I trouble you for a ride again, Frank?" the Professor asked.

"Sure, no problem Professor."

Abe Silver showed up at my office in the morning at 8:30. He had a couple of coffees in his hand and a bag of bagels. Where he'd found bagels in this town was a mystery to me. I thought to myself that I could get to like the little guy.

Flannigan had called earlier to say that he had cleared things with his captain. He'd be there with another detective and there'd be a prowl car in the neighborhood as a backup. Silver and I went over our plan, which wasn't much, over the bagels.

As we were getting ready to head out he asked me, "Do you have a gun, Frank?"

I opened my coat to show the .45 automatic I had stuffed in a shoulder holster. I don't normally like to carry a gat. You start going around with a gun and people end up getting shot. One of them might be me. But I figured in this instance I'd make an exception. McClure and his crew meant business and even with Flannigan waiting in the wings we might end up needing some protection. A model 1911 Army Colt is a brutal, primitive weapon, but it has a lot of stopping power. A .22 can kill you dead just as much in the right hands, but it just doesn't have the same potential for intimidation.

"What about you?"

"Me?" Abe shrugged. "I'm just a glorified claims adjuster. What would I be doing with a pistol?"

I didn't think less of him for that. I'd rather have an unarmed guy at my back than one who didn't know how to handle the weapon he carried.

We drove over to the trucking company's warehouse in Abe's car. I had to admit the Pontiac was a lot more comfortable than my Chevy. The inside was spotless. The springs in the seats weren't broken, either. Now that I had a little money, I'd have to think about upgrading my ride. But that was for later.

I let Abe take the lead. It was his show. He looked the part, nice crisp suit, not new but good quality. He had his briefcase in hand. He looked like a guy who was just there to fill out the paperwork.

We entered the office. It was a big room with a half dozen paper cluttered desks. Calendars with pictures of semi-trucks hung on walls that looked like they hadn't been painted in a while. The last coat might have been beige. Along one wall was a big black-board with what looked like drivers and destinations chalked in. It was about what you'd expect for a trucking company.

There was a bleached blonde sitting at the reception desk. A typewriter sat on the desk, but it was wearing a dust cover that look as if it hadn't been off in a while. Somehow, I got the feeling she was a recent addition. I couldn't imagine her being hired by Herbert DuVille.

Abe handed her his card. "If I could speak to whoever is in charge?"

The blonde knew enough to work the buzzer of the intercom. "There are two gentlemen from the Mid-Continental Insurance Company, here, Mr. McClure."

A couple of seconds later a big guy stepped out of a office in the back of the room. I noticed as he was walking towards us that he was wearing expensive hand-made Italian shoes.

Abe handed him another one of his cards. "Abe Silver, Mid-Continental Insurance. I'm here in reference to the DuVille claim."

"What of it?" McClure asked. For a guy trying to talk the insurance company out of a million bucks he wasn't being overly friendly.

"Well, Mr. McClure, you understand that with a claim of this size, the company wishes to exercise its right to examine the scene of the accident. To look for signs of negligence, safety violations, that sort of thing. I'm sure there is nothing like that in this case, but I have to go through the motions. There are forms that have to be filled out, reports. That sort of thing. I won't take up any of your time. We'll just look around so I can complete the paperwork."

I had to admit that Abe had the weasel-voiced nebbish act down pat. Even I might think he was harmless if I didn't know better.

"And if I say no?" McClure retorted.

"Well, in that case, Mr. McClure, I would have to put that in my report. I'm afraid that might mean the claim would be delayed. It might even be denied. The company is very particular about such things."

"And this mug?" he said nodding at me. "What's he doing here? He doesn't look like an insurance man to me." He knew who I was, alright.

The question didn't seem to faze Silver at all. "This is Mr. Slade. He's a private investigator. The company employs him as a consultant on occasions. He's just here so that we can complete our examination in a minimum amount of time."

I could see the wheels going around inside McClure's head. He was in a spot, and he knew it. Sooner or later the fallout from the jewelry store heist would come to roost. The best thing he and his partner could do would be to wind things up. But a million bucks is still a million bucks and it was hard to leave that kind of money on the table. The best thing he could do would be to let Abe go about his business so that he could collect on the policy before he blew town.

"I don't know why you need a private dick to investigate an unfortunate industrial accident, but I guess that's your business. Go ahead and take your look around. The warehouse is through those doors. Just don't get in the way—and make it snappy. I've got a shipping company to run here."

He spun on his heels and disappeared back through the door he had come out of.

"Well, we might as well get about it then, Mr. Slade," Abe said with a shrug. With a wink to the receptionist he said, "Good day, Miss."

The warehouse was what you'd expect, a large, high space dimly lit by big bulbs in metal reflectors suspended from the ceiling. A row of windows high up on the walls that looked like they hadn't been washed in years added a minimal amount of illumination. Stacks of boxes and cartons were spread out over the concrete floor separated by aisle marked out in yellow paint. In the distance a fork lift could be heard shifting some of the freight.

We followed one of the aisles into the middle. Stopping, Abe opened his briefcase and pulled out a small notebook which he proceeded to consult. If he was trying to look like some innocent pencil-pusher, he was doing a pretty good job of it. Snapping his briefcase closed again, he pointed off towards the southwest corner and said, "This way, I think." I followed like he was the boss.

We didn't make a bee-line for the corner, but kind of ambled, stopping here and there to examine various stacks of boxes. Every once in awhile, Abe would stop and write something down in his notebook. The guy should have been actor; he was a natural.

We eventually worked are way to the corner where there were a number of stacks of cartons containing electronics. Each of them had printed in big letters some cryptic designation like "CR-1020-V" and "TP-3003" along with the logos of various Japanese companies. It was a perfect place to hide a box labeled "X-300." In fact it was a perfect place to hide a dozen such boxes, for piled behind a stack of boxes of hi-fi speakers was tower of cartons reaching up about eight feet, each one imprinted with the legend "X-300."

"Now what?" I asked Abe.

"Check the shipping labels, of course," he said. He opened his briefcase again and pulled out a little flashlight, and began to check the white paper shipping slip that had been pasted on the side of each carton. Finally, after examining the labels starting from the top he stopped at the fourth from the bottom.

"This one, I think. You're taller than I am. Start clearing off the ones on top."

I did as he asked, removing the boxes and building a new stack next to the old one until I had worked my way down to the box he had indicated. Abe reached into his pocket and came out with one of those little Swiss Army knives, the ones with a dozen or so blades, screw drivers, corkscrews and such. Working carefully he slit the tape holding it shut.

Folding back the flaps he revealed a clear plastic envelop with what looked like an instruction manual sitting atop a Styrofoam shell that looked just like what you would expect protecting a piece of stereo equipment.

"Looks like a bust. Do you think the Professor played us for patsies?"

"Lift up the plastic, Frank," Abe said, unperturbed.

I did as he asked. Nestled in the lower shell was a glittery mass of jewelry, rings, necklaces, bracelets. I'm no expert on such things, but they looked like the real deal, more than a million in hit ice.

Abe plucked a necklace from the pile. It had a dozen or so links each set with a diamond from which dangled the biggest stone I'd ever seen. He consulted his notebook.

"This matches the description of one of the items taken from the jewelry store. Retail price, thirty thousand. I've got the complete inventory here, but I think this is enough."

"Find what you're looking for?"

I spun around reaching into my coat for my gun, but I stopped when I saw the speaker. It was McClure, and he was holding a chrome plated automatic that was pointed at my chest. There was another guy with slicked back hair standing next to him. He was holding a revolver. I assumed it was Trentino.

"I'll take that, Slade." Trentino stepped forward, and brushing aside my arm he reached in to relieve me of the .45 I was carrying.

"You realize, Mr. McClure, that if anything happens to us, your claim won't be allowed," Abe said. I had to admire the guy. He was taking it all pretty calmly. I wondered where the hell Flannigan was.

"That's a risk we'll have to take, Mr. Silver," McClure responded.

Trentino asked, "So what do we do now, Rory?"

"Easy. We take these two, stuff them in a box and put them on a truck to someplace—say, Peoria. With luck it could be weeks before the bodies are discovered. By that time we'll have blown this burg and sipping Mai Tai's on a beach somewhere where they don't have extradition."

"What about the cops?"

"They've got nothing on us, Tony. The ice will be out of here tonight. If they ask about these two, we can say they came and left. It's simple. All we have to do is knock these two off and stuff them in a crate. Turn around, Slade. You can go first."

As I turned, the only thing going through my mind was how mad Janet would be if I missed the wedding.

Suddenly there was the sharp bark of a pistol. Amazingly, I wasn't dead. I snuck a peek around and saw McClure laying on the ground. Abe Silver was holding a short barreled .38 revolver, the kind they call a "Banker's Special." It was pointed at Trentino who seemed too stunned to move. I reached over and grabbed the gun from his hand and retrieved my own .45 from his pocket. In the distance I could hear the sound of flat feet running. It was music to my ear.

"I thought you said you weren't carrying a gun?" I asked Abe.

"No. What I said was 'What would I be doing with a gun?' I think this answers that question." Abe's got a strange sense of humor sometimes.

I didn't have time to say anything more because Flannigan and another plain clothesman had come up with guns drawn. A couple of uniforms followed close behind. Trentino and McClure were in cuffs in a couple of seconds. McClure was still alive; Abe had only hit him in the shoulder.

"You might be interested in this, Lieutenant," one of the cops said pointing at the open carton.

"I think you'll find the contents will match the list of the items stolen in the jewelry store heist," Abe said. "That should give you grounds for a warrant to inventory this warehouse. I suspect you might find a few other things that have gone missing as well.

"I have a feeling you're right," Flannigan responded just shaking his head.

McClure got life with no parole. Trentino rolled over on McClure for a reduced sentence. They caught the two guys that did the heist in a motel room in Jacksonville. Neither one survived the shootout that ensued.

The insurance company was very happy, as well they should be after getting off the hook for two million. They showed their gratitude in the form of a check for fifty G's to one Frank Slade. They even kicked in another ten grand to the Professor for "information leading to a recovery." No comment was made about where the information came from. Abe used some of his connections and the Professor is taking his act to the Catskills this summer. No word on if Kenny is going with him.

Mid-Continental didn't forget about Abe, either. He's been named Regional Director of Claims Investigations or something like that. Didn't sound like much to me, but it seemed to make him happy. His stock with his relations seems to have gone up, too, for solving the murder of his cousin. From what I hear there are quite a few mothers trying to get introductions to Abe for their daughters.

Mrs. DuVille came out okay, as well. The courts ruled that because Mr. DuVille had been murdered, the clause in the partnership giving McClure and Trentino ownership was invalid. Of course, she didn't want to run the company, but Abe put her onto a competitor that made a very generous offer. She's thinking of opening an institute for psychic research with the proceeds.

Even Lt. Flannigan got something out of it. Solving the jewelry store murders made him the fair haired boy of the press, and the rumor is that he's next in line for Captain of Detectives when the current captain retires the end of this year.

So everybody ended up living happily ever after, except maybe for Herbert DuVille. He hasn't made a return engagement since the night of that last séance, so nobody has been able to ask him. But I hope he's happy with the way things turned out, wherever he is.

So, do I believe in ghosts? A good question. Was it all some con on the part of the Professor? He would never admit anything one way or the other. He claims he was off in a trance the whole time DuVille was supposedly showing up during the séances. It's hard to see how he could have known about all the particulars like the key in the barbershop and which box had the jewelry hidden in it. That would have taken some kind of inside knowledge.

But to think that Herbert DuVille was actually speaking to me from "the other side," that's a big leap of faith. I'm not sure I'm ready for that. But then, who am I to question such things? After all, I'm not even sure that I'm real, and not just a product of old Ezekial O. Handler's imagination. So here I am again, left with more questions than answers.

What I do know is that I'm not going to let it eat at me this time. After all, I've got a wedding to a beautiful woman coming up in a few weeks, and I've got more money than I've ever had before sitting in my bank account. Why should I worry about things beyond my understanding?

The Fictional Detective and the Haunted House

The Fictional Detective and the Haunted House

This story starts the way these kind of stories always do, a man sitting in a dingy, low-rent office in a run-down building in a part of town that isn't nearly as nice as it used to be. It's late afternoon, the sky is cloudy with portents of a late autumn drizzle that would be more cold than wet. The thin gray light slipping through the dirty windows fall on a décor that hasn't changed in fifty years, a wooden desk with a matchbook evening up one leg, a couple of steel file cabinets against the wall, a desk chair on rollers behind the desk and a pair of wooden chairs that are more comfortable than they look placed carefully in front of it.

There is a half full bottle of rye on the desk next to a clean desk, but lately that has been more for the effect than use. There are a few new things in the office, a serviceable typewriter placed center front on the desk and a coffee maker sitting on one of the file cabinets. There has been one other change, too; on the frosted-glass of the office door the word "Detective" has been scraped off and replaced with "Writer" in lettering that doesn't quite match the previous caption. The name above it, "Frank Slade," has remained the same.

Slade, that's me in case you haven't figured that part out yet, is still there, too, staring into space and trying to avoid work. That part is the same, but in other ways I've changed, too. Marriage will do that to you, particularly when the person you're married to is a woman like Janet Nielson. Note that I didn't say dame. Janet may be many things, but a dame she is not. She is one class act, long and lean with curves in all the right places and blonde hair curling to her shoulders. She knows how to dress and how to act. I've discovered she even knows how to cook. It had been her suggestion that I give up the P.I. racket and try my hand at writing. With a package like that can you blame a guy for taking the hint?

With the contacts she had as the mistress of the late Ezekial O. Handler, author of such works as *The Uncorrupted Corpse,* she had managed to convince a publisher into giving me a three book contract. Not that my association with solving the writer's murder hadn't helped. That was why I was sitting in the old office, with a typewriter on the desk, a box of blank paper sitting next to it, and a hefty advance for the first book sitting in the bank. Now all I had to do was start putting some words down on paper.

Instead, I found myself staring at the office door just as I had in my days as a private investigator hoping that someone would walk through it so I could pay next month's rent. Not that I needed the money now. The book advance and what Handler had left Janet in his will more than met our not particularly modest needs. But the writing was going nowhere and I felt the need of stimulation.

That's why, when I heard the sound of high heels in the hallway outside the office, my ears pricked up. I could see the shadow cast by the hall light against the frosted glass of the door of a statuesque dame as she hesitated at the threshold. I expected her to move on looking for the photographer or dentist that shared the floor with me, but instead she knocked. A very firm knock.

"Come in, the doors unlocked," I called out, even though I knew I'd only end up explaining how I wasn't a private dick anymore. Still, it pays to be polite, and I needed the distraction.

Distraction it proved to be, though not the way I had expected. Distraction is a good description for Josephine LaTouche, also known as Joseph Jaworski. She/he is the headliner at the Blue Angel, a cabaret that aspires to the decadence of Berlin between the wars but mostly comes off as just camp. On stage, she has the voice and presence, and strategically placed padding, to pull it off, a six foot vision of femininity the like of which few women can match. That day she was dressed more modestly in a snug gray skirt and a pink sweater that was too tight for modesty, topped with an auburn wig.

I knew Josephine because she had been a friend of Handler's. As far as I knew the relationship had been platonic, but the writer had trusted her enough that he had left a clue to his murderer with her, a clue that she had handed to me. Along with Janet, myself and a few other people, she was part of that weird world that Handler claimed he had concocted as part of his plan to bring his murderer to justice. But that's another story, and to this day I'm not sure I believe it despite the fact that I was at the center of the whole thing. Whatever the case, those events had created a bond between the people involved, so much so, that when Janet and I were married, Josephine had sung at the wedding.

"Jo. What brings you to this part of the world? Slumming?"

"Nice to see you, too, Frank," LaTouche replied in a warm contralto. "I called the apartment, but Janet said you were down here. I thought that you'd have given up this rat-trap."

"I had the rent paid for another month, and I found that I just can't get in the proper frame of mind to write at home. Too many distractions, if you get what I mean. Besides it's too clean. I thought this place would have a better atmosphere for writing detective novels."

"So how's that working out for you, Frank?"

"I've got the typewriter, I've got the paper. I even have a fresh ribbon in the drawer. It's the words that seem to be giving me trouble."

"Sorry to hear that, Frank. At least when I get a mental block I can go out and buy a dress or a new pair of shoes."

"Oh, I figure it won't be bad once I get started. And I've got a couple of months before the publisher is going to start asking where the book is. But I gather that you didn't come down here just to discuss my literary travails?"

"You *are* still the detective, Frank," Jo said with a laugh. "The fact is, that I've got a bit of a problem, and I didn't know who else to turn to."

"I'm out of the detective racket, Jo. That was part of the deal with Janet."

"I know, Frank. But this isn't that kind of problem, really. Not a criminal sort of thing. Besides, I talked it over with Janet when I called. She was very sympathetic, and said she had no objections to your helping me out."

I could see where this was going, the girls getting together behind my back. I bowed to the inevitable. "Well, as long as it's okay with Janet. What's your problem, Jo?"

"My Aunt Denuta died recently. She and I were always real close. She always encouraged my theatrical ambitions. She even came to see the show a few times. Well, she married my Uncle Stanislaw, that's Stan Dombrowski. Uncle Stan did real well for himself. He owned Stan's the Man Plumbing. He made quite a lot of money which he left to my Aunt Denuta when he died. They never had any kids of their own, so when she died, she left me their house. It's a real nice place, one of those big old Victorian house, and it's worth quite a lot of money, I gather."

"I'm sorry to hear about your aunt, but it sounds like you made out okay. I don't see what I can help you with."

"The place is way too big for me to live there all by myself, and frankly, Frank, it's a bit of a horror. You know what those Victorians are like, all the gingerbread and small rooms and things. So I want to sell it, but there's a little bit of a problem—"

"I'm not sure how I can help, Jo. I don't know much about real estate—"

Jo took a deep breath that caused her bosom to heave underneath the pink sweater. "It's like this, Frank. The house is haunted. That's why I can't sell it. I was hoping that maybe you could look into it and, well—"

"—unhaunt it?"

"Yeah, that's what I was thinking," Jo said with just the right inflection. She watches a lot of old movies and has all the dialog tricks down pat.

"It's a little out of my line, Jo. It sounds a lot more like something for the Professor." Professor Longwell was an indifferent stage magician that was occasionally on the bill at the Blue Angel. He was also something of a genuine psychic medium. At least I'd never been able to catch him faking it during the séances I had witnesses as part of my last case.

"I thought of that, Frank. But he's still not back from the Catskills. You're the only hope a poor girl's got." Jo batted her artificial eyelashes at me. I've always been a soft touch with the dames. Besides, Jo is quite an actor.

"Okay. I'll see what I can do. But how do you know the place is haunted?"

"I've seen them, myself. The ghosts, I mean."

"There's more than one?" I asked skeptically

"Yes. Of course," Jo replied. She took a moment to recover where she was at in her story. "Yes. There's two at least. Maybe three. I didn't get a good look."

"And when did you see these ghosts?"

"I spent a night in the house. Right after the will was read. But never again. I'm a big girl, Frank, and there's not a lot of things I'm afraid of, but ghosts are one of them. Anyway, I went to spend the night in the house. It was after my last show, so I didn't get there until after one. I went to bed, but about an hour later I heard these noises, like someone was in the place. So I got up to check it out. That's when I saw them. Two ghosts, plain as day."

"And how did you know they were ghosts?"

"I could see right through them. Just like in the movies."

"Are you sure you didn't just imagine all this, Jo? After all, it was late, you were tired. You probably had had a drink or two at the Blue Angel."

"I saw them, Frank! I didn't imagine it. Other people have seen them, too. The place has a reputation. That's why I can't sell it. Not until I can get rid of the ghosts."

"Okay. You saw the ghosts. Other people have seen them, too. What did these ghosts look like?"

"They were two men. Dressed in suits with hats, you know like out of the twenties, except they were all sort of translucent and glowing white like."

"And what were they doing when they saw you?"

"They were just walking around the house. It was like they were searching for something."

"Did they give any sign of noticing you?"

"No. But I just stood there on the stairs like I was frozen stiff. They walked down the hallway towards the back of the house until I couldn't see them anymore."

"Let me get this straight, then. There were these two guys who looked like they might be from the twenties, and they were just walking around the house and they didn't appear to notice you. Doesn't sound too gruesome to me. Are you sure you just can't learn to live with them?"

"Could you? Besides, I don't want to live with them. What I want is just to sell the place. I could really use the money. I'm not getting rich at the Blue Angel, that's for sure. A girl has got to think about her future. I'm not going to be able to strut my stuff for ever, Frank."

"What about your aunt and uncle, then? Didn't they have troubles with these ghosts?"

"Well they did, when they first moved in. And that was thirty years ago. The ghosts were already there at that time. That's why my Uncle Stan bought the place, because he got a good deal on it. But, see, my aunt and uncle were good Catholics. They had a priest come in and do an exorcism or something. That kept the ghosts at bay while they lived. But now that they're both dead, the ghosts have come back. Oh, what am I going to do, Frank?"

"Like I said, Jo, ghosts are kind of out of my line. But I'll see what I can do for you. Have you got a spare key you can give me so I can check the place out?"

"Sure, Frank. Right here." She reached into her purse and pulled out a key ring with a half-dozen keys. It had a little paper tag attached to it with the address written on it. "I got this from the lawyer. This one here opens the front door. I'm not sure what all the other are for."

I took the keys and stuffed them in my pocket.

"Thanks, Frank. I really appreciate this. You're one swell fellow."

"What are friends for, Jo?"

"Well, it's getting late, and I have to get ready for tonight's show. Say hello to Janet for me." She got up to leave. I found myself standing as well as I watched the wiggle of her hips as she walked out of the office. Not for the first time I found myself wondering at what a strange world I had found myself in.

After she was gone, I didn't feel like staring at the blank sheet of paper in the typewriter any more. Besides, Janet would have dinner waiting for me at home. Our marriage was recent enough that the idea of having a home, let alone one kept by a beautiful woman was still somewhat foreign to me. A year earlier, I had been a two-bit P.I. living in an apartment over a garage surviving on canned beans and cheap diner food. Before that—well, let's not go there because even I'm not too sure of my more distant past. Handler, in one of his posthumous letters, had claimed that I, along with all those that I held near and dear, was just a product of some magical mojo that he had worked as part of a scheme to catch his killer. That was a lot to accept, only it explained too many things. It had bothered me for a while to the point that I had almost disappeared in a bottle, until finally I had decided my past didn't matter; that it was the future that was important, and my future looked bright indeed.

If Ezekial Hander had been responsible for creating me as the instrument to bring his murderer to justice, I couldn't complain that he had left me with the short end of the stick. He had left Janet a fancy downtown condo, and between a fat insurance policy, a generous will and the publishing rights to his last few books she was set for life financially, and, as her husband, so was I. The doorman might still look at me with disdain, but it was my name on the mailbox.

Janet was in the kitchen when I walked through the door and the smells coming my way had never seen the inside of a can. For most women, being beautiful would be enough, but Janet can cook, too. She was dressed in a green sweater that complemented her blonde hair and slacks that were snug without being too tight. There was just a smudge of sauce on her pert nose. She was perfect, too perfect, the kind of woman that you only read about in detective fiction, but who am I to complain.

"Did Josephine get in touch with you?" she asked after I had licked the sauce off her nose. Except for having known Handler, the two of them had nothing in common, but somehow they seemed to have forged a bond. Maybe it was that neither posed a threat to the other. Maybe it was something else. Whatever the case was, the two could be thick as thieves at time.

"Yeah, she stopped in at the office."

"It sounded like she had a problem. Was it anything you could help with?"

That's what I mean about being thick as thieves. Janet had been against me staying a private eye, hence my so far futile attempts at being a writer. I can't say I blame her. It's a dangerous line of work and the pay is lousy. But here she was hinting that I should poke my nose into the singer's problems.

"It's not much of a problem. She inherited a house from her aunt. Some big old place that Jo wants to sell rather than live in, only she's having a problem unloading it and was hoping I could help her out."

"What does she think you can help with? You don't know anything about real estate, Frank."

"Well, it seems the reason no one will buy the place is that it's haunted."

"Haunted?" Janet said. There was a catch in her voice as she said it. Janet is a part of Handler's fantasy, too, and any hint of the supernatural gives her the shivers.

"Yeah. Seems there is a pair of transparent guys wandering the halls in the middle of the night. I'd chalk it up to some sort of urban legend except Jo claims that she's seen them herself."

"What does she think you can do about it, Frank?"

"I don't know, but she didn't really have anyone else to turn to. I thought I'd check the place out, see if I could spot any hanky-panky going on."

"Tonight?" she asked with a hint of alarm.

"Don't worry. I thought I'd wait till tomorrow morning when I could give the place the once over in the light of day."

"That sounds like a smart idea. Why don't you wash up. Dinner will be ready in a few minutes. And Frank—"

"Yeah, baby?"

"Be careful, won't you?"

"Always, Janet. I've got a lot to lose."

In the morning after breakfast I slipped the keys Jo had given me into my pocket and got the Chevy out of the garage. I was feeling ready to take on a whole host of apparitions. Bacon and eggs will do that to a man.

From the address, I knew the general neighborhood. It had been a fashionable district towards the end of the Victorian era where the successful and well off had built their palaces. It had been an age of beer barons and dry goods millionaires who had wanted to flaunt their newly acquired wealth and show that they were somebody.

I pulled up in front of what was one of the more modest of these residences. It was a three storey monstrosity, built in a dark red brick that was showing its age. There were plenty of crenellations along the roof line, lots of details encrusted with a century of pigeon droppings and even an honest to god turret. Ivy had wrapped its way around most of it. I could see how it had given Josephine the horrors.

By modern standards it was a big place, though I doubted that it had even a dozen bedrooms. It probably had a bathroom on every floor, too, and I bet the kitchen was in the basement. The yard was wrapped in a fence of ironwork that sported nasty looking spikes on top. The Victorians had had strange ideas of what constituted a welcoming home.

The gate on the front walk gave out an appropriate creak as I opened it. My entrance would have been more in keeping with the atmosphere of the place if it had been in the middle of a thunderstorm, but as it was, it was a bright, crisp morning with hardly a cloud in the deep blue sky. I whistled a jaunty tune as I marched up the walk to the front door which was reached after a flight of about half-a-dozen steps. The door was one of those things that are nearly big enough to walk a giraffe through, eight feet high and about four feet wide. The lock, though, had been recently oiled and turned easily when I inserted the key.

The layout was about what I had expected, a big entry hall running towards the back with a broad staircase leading up to the next floor. The ceilings were high, maybe twelve feet, which had the effect of making the rooms feel smaller than they actually were. There was a formal parlor to one side of the entry hall and a study or library opposing it. Farther back was a dining room big enough for twenty and another room that seemed to have been fitted out as a music room. None of the period details had been removed, so there was plenty of wainscoting and paneling and some ugly, dark wallpaper. The light fixtures looked as if they were the ones that had replaced the original gas fixtures back around 1900, and had lots of nooks and crannies and curlicues that would collect dust like crazy.

The house was furnished, but I couldn't get a good look at most of it, because everything had been covered with sheets to keep off the dust. The overall effect was plenty spooky, like walking into the set of a low budget horror movie. No wonder Jo wanted to unload the place.

The dust wasn't that thick on the floors, but it was thick enough to reveal footprints. There weren't that many, about what you'd expect if the place was being shown by a realtor, and included some that I recognized as Jo's size twelve high heels.

I did a walk-through of the first floor and didn't notice anything obviously amiss. As I was in the back of the house, I took the servant's stairs up to the second floor. This was more of the same, five bedrooms and a single bath complete with a claw-foot tub. What I assumed was the master bedroom used the turret as a sort of private sitting room. The sheets had been removed from the furniture which probably meant that this was where Jo had slept her one night in the place.

I opened the other rooms on the floor, but all were shrouded in sheeting. I tried to add up the number of sheets that had been needed to cover all the furniture, but gave it up when I got to a hundred. It must have cost a lot of money to be rich in the good old days.

The third floor had more bedrooms and another bath. The dust was thicker here with fewer footprints. None of the rooms were furnished and things had the look of having been shut up for decades. I guessed that Uncle Stan and Aunt Denuta hadn't had the need for more than five bedrooms.

The servant's stair led up to the attic to reveal a number of small bedrooms for servants. It looked as if it had taken a staff of a half-dozen or so to run the place when it was first built. Judging from the fact that there were no signs of heating or plumbing in the attic, life must have been pretty grim for the servants.

So far, I hadn't seen any signs of unusual activity, supernatural or not. I descended by the front staircase to the main floor. The kitchen, as I suspected was in the basement, along with the laundry, pantry, scullery and all the other little below stairs rooms of a well fitted Victorian house. Actually, basement was something of a misnomer as the floor was only a foot or two below the outside grade. Judging from the appliances, the kitchen had been modernized sometime in the 1950s, but the rest of the ground floor rooms were pretty much as they had been at the turn of the century.

There was a proper cellar below the ground floor, but that seemed to be given over to an ancient furnace, coal storage and a wine cellar, which sadly proved to be empty. Stan and his wife must have been beer drinkers or teetotalers.

As I stood in the hallway after my inspection, I came to the conclusion that I wasn't any wiser as to the source of Jo's supernatural manifestations. What I had found was a house far too large and antiquated for modern times. My personal recommendation to Jo would be to either find someone willing to do a complete remodel or better yet, tear it down and build something new. The property that the house stood on was prime real estate, a good three-quarters of an acre within a few minutes of the heart of the city. As such, it was probably worth more as an empty lot than with the house on it.

I felt that I had wasted most of the morning which left me wondering how to waste the rest of the day. I have to admit that I was finding Jo's haunted house problem more interesting than my attempts to write a detective novel. The house might not have revealed any secrets, but maybe that was just because I had been looking in the wrong places. What I had to find out was about the house's past. If there were rumors going around that it was haunted, then there must be something in the house's history that had inspired those rumors.

Now this is the point where most writers would head for the nearest library and immerse themselves in newspaper archives looking for accounts that might shed light on the matter. I had neither the time or the inclination to indulge in such research. What I did have was an acquaintanceship with Ed Stone.

Ed Stone is an old school crime reporter, the kind of guy that had been the life's blood of local newspapers back in the day before the news had been condensed into a ten minute TV segment leading into the weather and sports. He had been covering crime in the city for over forty years, and the only reason he hadn't retired was that there was nothing else that he liked to do better. We'd crossed paths on occasion back in my days as a private dick and had come to the mutual realization that each could act as a resource for the other.

Luckily, when I gave him a call, he was at his desk. I outlined my interest and he seemed intrigued by the problem. He agreed to meet me for lunch and gave me the name of a local tavern a few blocks from his paper's offices.

The bar had the look of having been there since before the passage of the Volstead Act, and not having changed much since. There were a few concessions to modernity such as the TV set over the bar which one assumed was only turned on during sporting events. There was an impressive mahogany back bar against the side wall, a long bar in front of it, and a few tables against the opposite wall as a concession to the more gentile patrons.

Ed was standing at the bar nursing a beer when I came in. Recognizing me silhouetted against the bright light of the doorway he called out, "Frank Slade, as I live and breathe," which was surprising as we had just talked on the phone less than thirty minutes earlier, but Ed was that kind of guy, hearty and outgoing with a lifetime of newspaper clichés on the tip of his tongue. The fact that he could still manage to be cheerful after a lifetime of staring at corpses was an indication of his success as a reporter.

"Beer?" he asked. I nodded agreement. "I'd recommend the rueben if you're hungry. It's the real deal."

"Sure, sounds good."

He motioned to the bartender, ordered two of the sandwiches and a brace of beers, then finished the one he had been drinking in one long swallow. When the bartender placed the beers on the bar he picked one up and dropped off of his stool.

"Let's grab a table for some privacy." This seemed unnecessary as there were only a two other patrons in the place and they were at the other end of the bar, but it was fine with me. I picked up the other beer and joined Ed at the closest table.

"So, do you know anything about this place I told you about?" I asked after we got situated.

"Sure, I know 'em all. It was built in the early 1880's by a grain merchant, but he didn't live there very long. He lost all his money in one of the crashes in the 1890's. After that it was bought by a doctor who had made some money with a patent medicine of some sort, a Dr. Schumway. He died during the big influenza epidemic after World War I. His widow sold the place. This is where it get's interesting—"

We were interrupted at that point by the bartender plopping two plates on the bar. I fetched the sandwiches, which I have to admit looked as good as Ed claimed, corned-beef piled high on thick slices of rye bread topped with Swiss cheese, Russian dressing and coleslaw. The corned-beef was sliced paper thin without much fat while the rye was dense and chewy with caraway seeds.

Ed didn't resume his story until he had polished off the sandwich.

"So you were saying about it getting interesting—" I prompted.

"Yeah. The guy that bought it was Augustus Wenzel, Fat Augie they called him. He was a local bootlegger in the early days of prohibition before the big Chicago mobs took over. He had had the forethought to build a secret brewery in 1919 and made a bundle selling beer during the first few years of Prohibition. That's how he could afford your friend's house."

"Well—and I think this is what has a bearing on your problem—like I said, he made a bundle, and the rumor got around that he had hidden most of it in the form of gold coins somewhere in the house. There was another rumor that two guys that worked for him broke into the house one night to look for it. It's said that Augie caught them red-handed and shot them both dead. It's also said, according to the same story, that he buried the two of them in the cellar. Nothing was ever proved, but the two of them were never seen again. Back then, the cops didn't much care if hoods knocked each other off. A couple of months later Fat Augie was caught in a Tommy-gun crossfire with a rival mob and killed. Title to the house passed to the county three years later when no one paid the taxes on it. The stock market crash happened soon after, and the house, which had been something of a white elephant before became unsalable during the Depression. Finally, just before the war a developer bought it at auction, but couldn't do anything with it while the war was on. Afterwards it changed hands a few times, but no one lived in it until Stan Dombrowski bought it for a song in the early fifties. He and his wife fixed if up and lived there until they both passed away."

"It's an interesting story, Ed, but I don't see how anything that you've said is relevant."

"Don't you get it, Frank?" Ed said, like I was an idiot child. "Two hoods killed on the premises and buried in the cellar? Fat Augie's treasure? Of course there were rumors. To start with, Augie was supposed to have hidden a million bucks in gold coins in the house. Even accepting that as an exaggeration, he *had* made a whole lot of money bootlegging that's never been accounted for. It must be somewhere. Why not the house? And the two hoods that disappeared. Maybe Augie did catch them trying to find that money and maybe he did shoot them and bury the bodies in the cellar. That's the kind of story legends are built on, Frank. Two tormented souls doomed to spend eternity searching the house for Augie's loot. You could make a movie of it."

I could tell that Ed's enthusiasm was getting the better of him, though I had to admit that it made a good story, maybe even something I could use in a book if I got really desperate.

"So, hasn't anyone ever gone looking for this treasure since? Or the bodies for that matter?"

"Sure, a number of people. But you got to remember that right after Fat Augie was killed the place was kind of in limbo, with guys with guns looking after it. I figure people were scared off by the mob ties until title passed to the county. By then some of the rumors of Augie's treasure had died down a bit. But they weren't forgotten. Every once in a while some bright guy would break in at night when they wouldn't be noticed. Always with the same results, they'd be scared off by ghosts. And the stories were always the same, two guys dressed like twenties hoods carrying guns and prowling the hallways."

"No one went in during the day?" I asked.

"Not that I know of," Ed conceded.

"I looked over the place this morning. I didn't see any signs of any search."

"Dombrowski was a practical kind of guy. I don't think he believed in the treasure or if he did, he probably figured someone had already gotten to it. When he bought the place, he patched up any of the damage the searchers had caused, and with people living in the house and it being so long after, no one has tried to find the treasure in maybe thirty years."

"So, if there *are* ghosts haunting the place, why didn't they ever bother Stan or Denuta?"

"How should I know, Frank?" Ed protested. "I'm a crime reporter not an expert on the heebie-jeebies. Maybe they didn't see the ghosts because they weren't looking for the treasure. Maybe they did see them and just ignored them. Maybe, because they were good Catholics they believed the priest when he said the ghosts were gone after he exorcised the place. How should I know?"

"Take it easy, Ed. I was just thinking out loud. How many people do you figure know about this treasure legend?"

"Probably not many anymore. Every once in awhile there'd be a story in one of the papers, but it's been years since the last one. There was a guy wrote a book a few years back, ok, maybe a dozen years ago. It was called something like *Haunted City* I think. It had all sorts of local ghost stories. I think there was a whole chapter about Augie's treasure and the mob ghosts."

"Well," I interjected, "just suppose someone happened to have read that book about the time that Denuta

Dombrowski's obituary appeared in the paper. Maybe they put two and two together and are trying to find the treasure, and maybe they're using the ghost story as a cover in case anyone interrupts them while they're at it."

"You've got no romance in your soul, Frank," Ed responded. "But I suppose that it's possible. But you said you hadn't seen any signs of anything."

"There were a bunch of footprints. I thought it might have been a realtor or someone. But maybe it's just because the treasure hunters are still in the scouting stage. They wanted to scare off Jo so they could work undisturbed."

"Be the realist, Frank. I say ghost mobsters and a lost treasure makes a much better story."

"I agree, Ed, but I've got a friend I'm trying to help out. Unless I can convince the world that there are no ghosts, she's not going to be able to sell the place."

"Well, let me know how it turns out, Frank. Either way, there's probably a good story in it for me. I've got to get back to work. Thanks for the lunch."

Ed was out of there like a shot, leaving me with the tab, but I didn't mind. I figured that I'd gotten my money's worth.

It was a little after one when I stepped out of the tavern's darkness into the bright afternoon. I realized that I was within walking distance of the main branch of the Public Library. A quick check of the card catalog there revealed that they did have a copy of the book *Haunted City* that Ed had mentioned. I found it on the shelves and spent the next half-hour reading the chapter on August Wenzel and his treasure. This pretty much confirmed the story Ed had told me and added a few details about various sightings of the ghosts. These were remarkably consistent in their descriptions of the apparitions. In the words of one of the people claiming to have seen the ghosts:

I saw the forms of two men walking down the main hallway of the house. They were glowing with a pale white light and you could see right through them like they were transparent. They were dressed like you see in pictures of gangsters from the Roaring Twenties. One was carrying a lantern and the other had a pickax. They didn't seem to notice me, but I didn't stick around.

Of course, the alleged witness had been in the house on a dare after a night of drinking, so even the author admitted that there was "some question of his reliability as a witness." Still, the description matched closely those of the other accounts.

The book went on to recount the story of the demise of Fat Augie and speculated on the nature and location of his treasure. As a budding author, I found the style a bit sensational and overblown. Of course, I hadn't had a book published at that time, so maybe I shouldn't have been so quick with my criticism.

After finishing the chapter, I returned the book to the shelves. It was still early afternoon, so I headed to my office to spend some time staring at my typewriter.

Surprisingly, an idea for a story had started to form in my mind. It involved a gangster's loot and an attempt to steal it. Ok, I admit that Fat Augie and his treasure were on my mind, but after a week of staring at a blank sheet of paper, I was ready to try anything.

By the time I knocked off writing at five, I had typed out twelve pages, nearly three thousand words worth of what would later become *Little Tony's Last Score*, my first novel. Feeling proud of myself, I headed home.

I was becoming preoccupied with the story of Fat Augie's treasure. I rationalized to myself that treasure hunters disguised as 1920s mobsters might offer an explanation for Josephine's ghosts, but really, it was the idea of finding hidden gold that was on my mind. Not that I wanted it for myself, mind, Janet and I had all the money we needed and Jo was a friend of ours. It was just the thought of solving a puzzle more than half a century old that had taken hold of my imagination.

It occurred to me that I hadn't really given the cellar much of an inspection. It had been dirty, the lighting had been bad, and I hadn't really been equipped for a detailed search. I decided to remedy that state of affairs.

Putting on the oldest set of my clothes that Janet hadn't seen fit to throw away when I had moved in, I equipped myself with a powerful flashlight and a short pry bar and headed back to the house.

This time, I decided to check out the exterior before entering. This wasn't that easy as much of the foundation was obscured by a barrier of overgrown shrubbery. A bed of pea-sized gravel lay up close against the house making it nearly impossible to leave a foot print.

It was when I had worked my way around to the back door, which must have served as the tradesmen's entrance for deliveries to the kitchen, that I found the first signs of something fishy. It was a stout door with a fairly modern, high quality lock operating a dead-bolt separate from the latch. I could see what appeared to be scratches from an inexpert effort to pick the lock. There were also marks where a pry bar had been inserted between the frame and the door in an attempt to spring the latch. That looked to have failed, too. Both the marks on the lock escutcheon and the frame looked to have been fairly recent, certainly within the last few weeks.

The burglars had failed in their attempts to break in through the door, but that didn't mean they had given up. I continued my circuit of the house, inspecting each of the windows for indications of their handy work. On the third window, which if my mental blueprint of the ground floor's layout was correct opened out into the scullery, I found a sign that they had been successful. This window, like all the other basement windows, had originally been protected by a set of iron bars, but sometime in the distant past, the bars seemed to have been removed. This left only a simple latch on the inside of the frame to secure the window. It looked like the burglars had slid a pry bar or some other flat piece of metal through the gap between the window and the frame and managed to undo the latch. From what I could see, it looked like they hadn't bothered to re-latch the window on their way out. Either they were planning on coming back, or just hadn't thought it worth their while.

For a moment I thought about following their path through the window, but then it occurred to me that I had a key. Why should I risk my neck and dignity climbing through a basement window when I could just as easily walk around to the door and approach it from the other side? I got up off my knees and did just that.

As I had suspected, the window opened out into the scullery just above a big soapstone sink. The window was hinged at the top and opened inward. There was a drop of a little over four feet into the sink. From there it would have been easy to get to the floor. The treasure hunters had been careful to not leave footprints on the floor, but they hadn't been as careful with the sink. I hadn't really had a reason to look that closely the day before, but when I directed the flashlight beam into the sink I could spot marks in the dust from two sets of footprints, one set about size eleven, the other maybe an eight and a half. Neither one were high heels, so that ruled out their having been made by Jo. Not that she would have had any reason to crawl in through the scullery window.

It was easy to see how they had gotten in. The question was what had they been up to once inside. It was time for me to check out the cellar.

I'd pretty much skipped it during my inspection the day before because frankly it was dirty and uninteresting. I'd have to approach it more seriously this time. The basement was laid-out with a long hall running front to back with various rooms opening off of it to either side. The kitchen was at the back of the house on the left looking down the hall from the front of the house with the pantry and scullery and laundry on the same side. The other side had the housekeepers quarters, the servants dining room and a couple of work rooms. The stairs to the cellar was between the scullery and the laundry.

There was a light switch just inside the door to the cellar and when I flicked it on a couple of bulbs lit up, one at the foot of the stairs and one off in the distance. What had been the wine cellar was to the left, storage and the furnace to the right. It was low ceilinged like most cellars of that period with the occasional beam forcing me to duck. Brick piers and wooden partitions broke up the space into a maze of little rooms.

Originally, the house had been heated with coal, but someone, probably Stan, had replaced it with a gas boiler. The old coal bunkers had been left in place, though, and though they had been emptied of coal, thick black dust still covered the floor. The floor itself, except for the coal bunkers was of fairly modern cement work, again, something that had probably been done when Dombrowski had bought the place. It effectively hid whatever the cellar had looked like back in Fat Augie's day.

That must have proved a problem for the treasure hunters. As I swung the beam of my flashlight around I could see spots where they had chipped at the floor with a pick. They seemed to have had a problem making up their minds as to the most likely spot, as they must have tried a half dozen places before giving up for the night. The low ceiling had caused them grief, too. I could see a couple of places where they had nicked the floor joists above with the pick on the back swing. These guys, whoever they were, looked to be amateurs.

There were certainly no signs that they had found Augie's hoard. They hadn't even penetrated the concrete of the floor. The question was, would they be back? I thought that they would. Sure, they might have gotten discouraged and given it up, but the lure of treasure can be mighty strong. They'd already crossed one line by breaking in. They probably keep at it until they had exhausted every possibility or were caught.

There wasn't anything more for me to do. I'd proved to my own satisfaction that Jo's ghosts were mere mortal treasure hunters. Whether Jo wanted to dig up the cellar in the pursuit of Augie's treasure was something for her to decide. Whichever way it went, there was no point in my getting any dirtier than I was already. I left the house, leaving the scullery window unlatched.

"So, what are you going to do?" Janet asked after I had repeated my story over dinner that night.

"I think that's up to Jo. She can report the break-in to the cops or she can act on her own. I was planning on asking her tonight."

"Tonight?"

"Yeah. I thought I'd catch her between shows at the Blue Angel."

"I don't know if I should let you go there alone, Frank. It might corrupt your morals."

"Not a chance, they were corrupted long ago, but if you want to tag along, that's fine by me."

The Blue Angel is literally a dive night club in the cellar of an older office building. Access is down a steep flight of stairs under a flickering neon sign. It's supposed to resemble the sort of place you could find in Berlin between the wars, like something you'd see in an old Marlene Dietrich movie or *Cabaret,* but of course on a more limited budget. Mostly it's guys dressed as girls or vice versa sitting at tiny tables drinking overpriced cocktails and watching the floor show. The place does have a sort of camp reputation, though, and not all of the clientele are transvestites. A lot of the acts are amateurs, but not all of them. Josephine LaTouche is the headliner and has been for several years.

I'd been in and out of the place enough that the maitre d' knew my mug. That and a five spot got us a table not too far from the stage. Of course, given the size of the room that could have described any of the tables. The "girl" on stage was Josephine's understudy. She had a good voice and didn't look too bad in a dress, but she lacked Jo's flair.

The waiter came and I ordered a bottle of cheap champagne and three glasses. Fortunately for us, the act on stage was in her final number. She exited to a smattering of applause and the M.C. announced that Miss LaTouche would be taking the stage in a few minutes. In the interlude the waiter arrived with the champagne and poured two glasses. Janet made a face when she took her first sip, but her manners were too good for her to comment.

The house lights dimmed and when they came back up, there was Josephine standing behind the microphone with the spotlight on her. You wouldn't think a guy nearly six-feet tall would look good in an evening gown, but Jo knows how to pull it off. Tonight she was wearing a tight, floor length, red sparkly number, a shoulder length blonde wig and white opera gloves. She waved to the audience and then broke into her first number in a throaty alto with hints of Sarah Vaughan. The background noise in the club dropped to a hush.

Jo worked her way through her set list, mostly show tunes and old jazz standards. She was backed by the house orchestra, a quintet of piano, bass, drums, saxophone and a guitar player that doubled on clarinet and trombone when called for. They weren't half bad, which, considering what the Blue Angel pays, is an indication of how many decent gigs there are for that kind of music.

It was interesting to watch Janet during the show. She wasn't quite sure whether to respond with appreciation or jealousy.

Jo knows how to work the material and work the crowd. By the time she finished the forty-five minute set with her signature closing number, "Lili Marlene," she had the crowd eating out of her hand, especially when she sang a verse in German. She gave one encore and then descended from the stage.

Sitting down at our table, she poured herself a glass of champagne and tossed it off in one long gulp.

"Singings thirsty work, Frank. Thanks for coming out to see me, Janet."

"You were marvelous, Jo," Janet said sincerely.

"So kind of you to say so. You said you wanted to talk to me, Frank. About the house I take it?"

I outlined what I had found out, including the evidence of a break in. Jo seemed unconvinced.

"I don't doubt what you're saying, Frank, but what I saw that night wasn't two guys pretending to be ghosts. They were real ghosts. I could see right through them. I've been in show business long enough to know a stage illusion when I see one."

"Can you be sure? It was late at night and you were probably half asleep—"

"I didn't imagine it, Frank," Jo interrupted. "What I saw were ghosts. And don't tell me there are no such thing. You've been involved with some pretty weird stuff yourself, Frank, to say such things can't happen. The Professor told me all about that séance business."

Jo had a point. I'd never made up my mind about that case, whether Longwell had been playing me or had really been channeling the spirit of Herbert Deville. It had spooked me at the time and I was glad when it was settled the old fashioned way, with a .38.

"Sure, Jo, but the fact is someone had been breaking in and digging up the cellar. They might do some real damage if they're not stopped."

"So what are you proposing to do about it? Go to the cops?"

"Without more evidence, the police aren't going to do much. They might send someone out to look at the window, but all they're going to say is that some kids broke in, and then they'll ask if anything was taken, and I'll have to say, no. Then they'll file a report and it will be forgotten."

"And so? What about Fat Augie's treasure?"

"An alleged treasure that no one has found in fifty years? That'll just give them a good laugh at my expense."

"So what *are* you planning to do, then?"

"Well, if you want to pursue it, I thought I'd stake out the place at night and try to catch them in the act as it were."

"OK. But what about the ghosts? I need to get rid of those ghosts, Frank. Otherwise, I'm never going to be able to unload that house."

"If the ghosts show up, Jo, I'll ask them to move on. How's that?"

"You don't believe me, Frank, do you? After all we've been through, you don't believe me!"

"Look, Jo. I believe you saw something. I'm just not sure it was ghosts. And even if it were, I'm not sure what I could do about them. It's a little out of my line—"

"How can you say that, Frank, after the séances and all the little notes Zeke left you after he was dead?"

"Well, if I see the ghosts for myself, maybe that will change my mind—"

That didn't seem to mollify Jo. She poured herself another glass of champagne and tossed it off in a huff.

It was at that point that Janet broke in:

"Isn't it true that ghosts don't just hang around? If that was the case, we'd be overrun with ghosts. But there is usually some sort of traumatic event that ties them to the place they haunt."

"Yeah, in the stories."

"And if August Wenzel did kill those two men—"

"Yeah. I see your point," Jo said. "Fat Augie's knocking them off and burying them in the cellar probably qualifies as a traumatic event. You should listen to Janet more often, Frank. She's got a lot of sense."

"OK. Let's say for the moment that the ghosts are the two guys that Fat Augie caught and that he did shoot them and bury them in the cellar. What can we do about it?"

"Dig 'em up, that's what. They're probably mad as hell at not being given a real burial. Even gangsters got religion."

"But we don't know where they are buried, or even if they are buried in the house," I protested. "We don't even know for sure if they were killed. The story is just a rumor, Jo."

"Well, maybe we can contact them, get them to tell us where they are buried," Jo responded with feminine logic.

"If the Professor were here, we could hold a séance, but he's still out east."

"I guess we'll just have to do it ourselves," Jo said firmly.

"What do you mean by we?"

"If you're going to sit up in that house all night, I'm going to sit with you. If I saw those ghosts once, I can see them again."

"Jo, a stakeout isn't anyplace for a—"

"Don't say it, Frank. Don't say 'woman'. I'm nearly as tall as you and I've got more heft. I can take care of myself. After all, I've been fending off drunks in this place for years."

"I'm sorry Jo, I didn't mean—"

"You better not have. It's settled. It's too late tonight, and besides I've still got another show. But tomorrow, I can get Lulu to fill in for me during the second show. It's Thursday and that's always a slow night, anyhow. You can pick me up here at eleven. We can be to the house and in place by midnight, easy."

"OK. But dress appropriate, Jo, will you?"

"I'm no fool, Frank," Jo retorted.

"Wait a minute," Janet interrupted. "You two don't think you're going to stay in that house overnight alone, do you?"

"Don't worry, Janet, Frank's not my type," Jo replied saucily.

"That's not what I mean, Jo. I want to go with you."

I started to say something and then thought better of it. I knew better than to argue with her. Besides, Janet could take care of herself, too. She'd saved my life once by shooting a guy who was going to kill me. Like I said earlier, she's the perfect woman.

The next morning I went into the office as usual, but I couldn't keep my mind on writing. I was too preoccupied with that evening's activities. Not that I was really worried. The two treasure hunters looked to be too amateurish to give us much trouble. I wasn't really that worried about the ghosts, either. I wasn't even sure I believed in them, despite what Jo had said. She can be kind of excitable at times.

What was really on my mind was Fat Augie's treasure. Something about the rumors surrounding it just didn't make any sense to me. Burying loot might have been fine for pirates, but criminals tend to like keeping their wealth in a more mobile form in case they have to make a hasty departure. A million bucks in gold coins would be awfully heavy. And having to dig it up would take time, even if you knew where it was. There was also the fact that dozens of attempts had been made over the years to find it. The cellar must have looked like Swiss cheese before Stan had repaved the floor.

No, I reasoned, it was much more likely that Fat Augie had kept his fortune in a more liquid form, say something like large denomination bills or bearer bonds. Something that could be stuffed in a suitcase in a hurry if he had decided to go on the lam. With that in mind, it was more likely that there was a concealed safe hidden behind a secret panel or something. With all the paneling and wainscoting in that house, there were plenty of places where something like that could have been hidden. And if Fat Augie had taken the secret to his grave when he was gunned down, the loot might still be there. Stan Dombrowski hadn't made many modifications to the place when he had moved in outside of some improvements to the kitchen and cellar. Maybe he'd missed it because he hadn't been looking for it.

After an hour of trying not to think about it anymore, I gave up. My curiosity had gotten the better of me. I grabbed my pry bar, a rubber mallet and a couple of other tools and headed back to the house.

Four hours of thumping walls later, I hadn't uncovered any secret panels. I hadn't found any hidden catches or anything similar, either. I'd been all over the first and second floors, sounding for hollow panels. All I can say is that they don't build them like that anymore. It was getting late, too, and Janet was expecting me for dinner.

I was in the master bedroom suite, catching my breath before calling it quits, sitting in a chair in the sitting area in the turret. That's when I noticed something funny about the layout of that room. The walls on the inside didn't quite follow the exterior walls. It wasn't particularly noticeable. The architect who had planned it had been good at his job. But there was a kind of dead spot, maybe two feet wide and three feet deep where the turret connected to the rest of the house between the interior and exterior walls. In a modern house, I might have suspected it of being a chase for plumbing or electrical conduits, but the house had been built before either of those modern conveniences. Besides, the only plumbing in the floor above was a bathroom located at the rear of the house.

It was possible that it was just empty space, and maybe it had been that when the house was built. But if August Wenzel had been looking for a place to hide a safe, that dead zone would have made a great place of concealment.

It was really tempting to try and pull off the paneling right then and there, but as I said, it was getting late. Besides, I didn't want to tear the place apart without Jo's permission. Regretfully, I packed up my tools and headed home.

I had a quiet dinner at home with Janet, after which we made our preparations for the stakeout. Janet's ideas for appropriate attire seemed to owe their origins to Hollywood's concept of the fashionable cat-burglar, for she was dressed in trim black slacks, a black turtle-neck sweater and to top it off, a black watch-cap to conceal her blonde hair. All in all, I found the outfit quite fetching and regretted the fact that we had quite different plans for the evening than those that were forming in my head.

I was dressed much more casually, dark pants, dark shirt, and a black leather jacket. The only remarkable addition to my wardrobe was the shoulder holster I wore under the jacket and the .38 automatic that it held. Even as a private investigator I had rarely carried a gun, but with Janet and Jo to protect, I found the weight reassuring.

We drove Janet's car, a black Mercedes, to the Blue Angel. Not only would it be less noticeable in the neighborhood than my aging Chevy, but it was also more comfortable and certainly cleaner.

Jo was waiting for us outside the nightclub. As a concession to practicality, she was dressed in a skinny pair of jeans and a tight, dark sweater with a black scarf around her neck. She had chosen a short black wig with bangs, and in place of her normal spike heels was wearing boots with chunky heels less than two inches high. Looking at my companions, I thought that we were as likely to leave the treasure hunters helpless with laughter as to frighten them off. What the ghosts might think I couldn't even guess.

We parked the car a couple of blocks away from the house so as not to alert the burglars of our stakeout. It was a full moon, but thick clouds covered it during most of our walk to the house. It was looking like it would be an appropriate night for ghostly apparitions as the wind was gusting and it gave every promise of rain before midnight.

In order to be less obtrusive, I wanted to go in through the back door rather than the front porch. This was easier said than done, though, because the backyard of the house was pitch black with neither streetlights or lights from neighboring houses providing much in the way of illumination. I finally had to resort to my flashlight to provide enough light for us to find our way to the back door.

Once inside, I left the women in the kitchen while I checked out the scullery. As far as I could tell, the treasure hunters hadn't been back since my last visit. I did a quick search of the rest of the ground floor and opened the door to the cellar, but except for Jo, Janet, and myself the house appeared empty.

Returning to where I had left my companions, I said, "We might as well go upstairs and make ourselves comfortable. I didn't see any signs of either the treasure hunters or the ghosts."

"Don't make fun of the ghosts, Frank," Jo complained. "I know what I saw, and it wasn't burglars."

"Sure, Jo. I believe you saw something weird. It's just that I'm not convinced it was supernatural. In any case, we should go upstairs so the treasure hunters won't suspect anything."

I ushered them upstairs and into the music room. I had decided that it was the best place for our vigil. As it was towards the rear of the house, we could use a flashlight without having it seen from the street. It was also on the opposite side of the house from the scullery window, so that if our treasure hunters used that way in, they wouldn't be able to see us.

After we removed the sheets from some of the furniture, the music room proved comfortable enough. Janet and I sat on a small settee while Jo planted herself in an overstuffed armchair. Her biggest problem would probably be staying awake through the night.

Janet had thoughtfully packed a selection of sandwiches and a large thermos of coffee. Just another example of why I love that woman. There was a small lamp on a side table next to the settee. It must have had only a forty watt bulb, because when I tried the switch it provided just enough light for us to see our way around. I decided it wouldn't be much of a risk to leave it on, so I turned off the flashlight to conserve the batteries.

We had just gotten ourselves settled in when it started to rain. It was late in the season for a thunderstorm, but thunder it did, probably just to provide the proper atmosphere. Every once in a while a flash of lightening would throw crazy shadows across the room. Janet was pressing herself up against my side. Not that I was complaining, mind you.

"Anyone know a good ghost story?" I asked, trying to lighten up the mood.

"Don't go joking about that, Frank," Jo reprimanded. "You'll cast a negative aura or whatever. Remember, we want the ghosts to appear. That's probably the only way I'm going to be able to get rid of them."

"Sorry, Jo. It's just that this is starting to play out like some bad horror movie. A haunted house, a thunderstorm, next thing you know, the electricity will go out."

As if on cue, the lamp flickered and went out. I felt Janet's fingers tighten around my arm.

"See, Frank," Jo said. "That's what comes of making fun of the ghosts."

"It's just the storm, Jo," I replied, turning the flashlight back on. "It must have tripped a breaker or blown a transformer someplace."

I got up and looked out the window, but I couldn't see a thing. The blackout must have affected the whole neighborhood. I found some candles and a pair of candlesticks on the mantel over the fireplace. Lighting these, I turned off the flashlight again.

"Why don't you believe in ghosts, anyway, Frank?" Jo asked. "You know that some pretty strange things have happened to us. You can't deny that. And the Professor told me all about those séances you had where you were talking with that DuVille guy."

"It's not that I disbelieve in ghosts, Jo. It's that I haven't seen undeniable proof that they exist, and until I do, I have to act as if there were rational explanations for what happened."

"And the séances?"

"Hey, don't get me wrong, I like the Professor, but I'm still not sure that it wasn't him talking and not Deville. Maybe not even consciously. But all the words I heard were coming from his mouth."

Quietly, Janet interjected, "But Jo is right, Frank. There was something strange about how Ezekial knew enough about what was going to happen after his death, that he wrote it down so you could find it. I don't see how there can be a rational explanation for that. Can you?"

Now, the whole business surrounding the mystery of Handler's death is something that I can't explain, and the fact that I can't explain it is kind of a touchy subject with me. It goes to the very heart of my relationship with Janet, and for that matter our very existence, and to some extent that of a number of our friends, including Jo. At one point, it had almost caused me to drink myself to death. The only way I've found to cope with those events is to ignore the whole subject. But that's another story.

"Let's just leave it at if I see ghosts tonight, I'll believe it, but until then, there are a couple of guys who have been breaking into the house to look for Fat Augie's treasure, and I'm sure that they're not ghosts."

Janet knew enough about how I felt on the subject to drop it. In many ways, she felt the same way. Jo, however wasn't about to let the subject go. She was about to raise a another point when Janet held up her hand.

"Did you hear that?"

Just as she finished, there was a boom of thunder, and it was several seconds before things were quiet enough for us to hear what she was referring to. Then it came, a clatter and then the sound of footsteps coming from the basement below us.

"You two stay here while I check it out," I whispered. Jo was going to object, but when she saw that I had drawn my gun she stopped.

With my pistol in one hand and the flashlight in the other I crept out into the hallway. Fortunately, the carpet runner down the center of the hall made it easy for me to move noiselessly. I headed to the rear of the house where the stairway to the ground floor was. When I reached the steps I turned off the flashlight and descended the steps.

The only illumination came from the lightning flashes, and I had to pause between them until the next flash gave me enough light to make my way. I went past the kitchen and pantry. The scullery door was open, and I stepped inside. There was a chill in the room and the scent of ozone, that smell you get during electrical storms.

I took a chance and pushed the switch of the flashlight. In the narrow beam I could see two sets of muddy tracks leading from the sink beneath the windows. I felt a little better when I spotted them. Ghosts don't leave muddy footprints.

The tracks led away from scullery sink. There were no returning footprints. The treasure hunters were still in the house. I followed the trail out of the room and down the hall to where they disappeared behind the door to the cellar. Cautiously, I opened the door. I could see a light coming from the rear of the cellar. They probably had a lantern, probably thinking themselves safe in the cellar which was completely below grade and had no windows.

I could hear the murmur of two voices which sounded like they were coming from the back of the house where the coal bins were. I couldn't make out the words, but I could distinguish two voices, one gruff and deep, the other higher pitched. Gripping my pistol tighter, I started slowly down the steps.

It was the third step from the bottom that gave me away by creaking loudly as it took my weight. I froze in position. It was obvious that I had been heard for the voices stopped. I waited for what seemed an eternity, but was probably only a dozen seconds, then descended the remaining steps to the cellar floor.

That was when the light from their lantern went out. I still had my flashlight, though, and I slowly proceeded towards the rear of the house.

I've described how the cellar had been divided up into a number of small rooms by walls and the piers that supported the upper stories. One of the burglars must have been waiting behind one of them. I never saw him. All I remember is a flash of light as my head exploded, and then, darkness.

"Frank, wake up." It was Janet's voice.

"Is he alright?" That was Jo.

"He's been hit on the head, It must have knocked him out. I think he's ok, though. His pupils are reacting to the light." This latter comment came as Janet swung her flashlight into my eyes.

"Lay off the light. It hurts."

"Are you alright, Frank?" Janet asked.

"My head feels like someone dropped a safe on it."

"It's a good think you were wearing that stupid hat. It may have saved your life." Janet has a thing about my fedora. She says they're no longer fashionable. She's probably right, but I'd feel naked without it. After this, may she wouldn't complain.

"What happened?"

"One of them must have got the jump on me from behind. I followed their tracks down here, but they must have heard me on one of the stair treads. What are you two doing down here anyway? I thought I told you to stay upstairs."

"It's been over a half an hour, Frank. When you didn't come back we got worried."

"You shouldn't have risked it. These guys are playing for keeps. Where are they, anyway?"

"I don't know, Frank," Janet answered. "When we came down into the cellar, you were the only one here."

"They must be somewhere upstairs in the house, then. At least that settles it, Jo. It wasn't ghosts that you were seeing. It was just two crooks."

Jo and Janet looked at each other like they had a big secret and weren't sure how to tell me.

"That's just it, Frank," Janet said in the tone of voice she always uses when she has something serious to say. "We did see the ghosts. Both of us. Just a few minutes ago."

"They were creeping down the hallway just outside the music room. They headed up the front stairs to the next floor," Jo explained.

"That's when we decided that we had to find out what happened to you," Janet completed.

"Are you sure it wasn't just the two guys that mugged me?"

"The lights were off in the hallway, and they were glowing with a soft light," Janet said. "We could see through them, too."

"They weren't leaving no muddy footprints like those other two bums, either," Jo chimed in.

"Maybe we should get out of here, Frank," Janet said. "Are you able to walk?"

"Sure, I'm fine," I answered. I didn't feel fine, but I didn't want to let the girls know. The blow to the head had left me pretty woozy. I managed to pull myself up to a standing position, but when I bent over to pick up my gun from where it had fallen after I was hit, I almost found myself back on the floor.

"Just give me a few seconds to get my sea legs under me."

"Frank, you don't have to be a hero for me," Jo said. "This house isn't worth it. You're in no shape to fight off those crooks, let alone ghosts. I say we get out of here right now."

I was starting to think that maybe Jo had a point. My head was still throbbing violently and my sense of balance was acting wonky.

"Yeah, maybe you're right. We should at least call the police. If breaking and entering isn't enough to get them here, assault with a deadly weapon is."

We made our way to the steps. I was leaning on Jo with one hand and carrying the pistol in the other, though I would have been pure luck if I could have hit the side of a barn the way it was wavering around.

When we got up to the ground floor, I flipped on the lights. To my relief, they came on, flooding the hallway with light. The electricity must have come back on while I was laying there in the cellar.

"Look, more footprints," Jo said. Sure enough, the two treasure hunters had left a trail of mud and coal dust heading towards the rear of the house. We followed it to where they led up the servants stairs.

"Is there a phone down here?" I asked.

"I think I saw one in the servants' dining room," Jo answered.

I sat down in one of the chairs and let Janet make the call. I wasn't sure I would have been coherent enough to convince the dispatcher that I wasn't a drunk.

Janet must have spent five minutes on the phone repeating our story, getting louder with each repetition. Finally she hung up in disgust.

"They said they'll send a car as soon as they can, but it might be a half an hour, maybe more. It seems there are a lot of trees down from the storm and power outages all over town. Most of the police are busy directing traffic where the stop lights aren't working."

"Great," I responded. "Well we can sit here until they come, I guess."

"With those two crooks running around the house?" Jo replied. "Not to mention the ghosts. We've got the gun. I say we find those two hoodlums and give them what for."

"I think Jo is right, Frank," Janet said. She had the same grim look on her face that she had had when she shot Buckley before he had had a chance to plug me. "Those two know that we're in the house. I don't think we should give them the chance to sneak up on us."

"Ok. But maybe you should take the gun then, I'm not too sure of my aim right at the moment."

"Don't worry, Frank. I've got one of my own." She was holding a .45 automatic in her hand. It looked like the same one that she had used on Buckley. I don't see how she could have been carrying a gun that big in her purse, but there wasn't anywhere else she could have concealed it.

"Jo?" I said, offering my pistol to her.

"Not me, Frank. I don't like guns. You go around with one of them things and someone might get hurt. Meaning me."

"All right. Might as well get moving."

We headed up the steps to the main floor. The footsteps continued up the servants steps.

"Look, why don't we use the main staircase? It's bigger. It would be too easy to get trapped on these narrow steps."

"Whatever you say, Frank," Janet said.

"And let's turn on every damn light switch we pass. The darkness isn't doing us any favors."

"You don't have to argue with me about that, Frank," Jo said. "the more light the better as far as I'm concerned."

I didn't see any footprints on the central hall. The intruders hadn't gone that way.

As we passed the music room, Jo said, "This is where we saw the ghosts, Frank. They went this way."

I didn't feel like arguing the point. Maybe they had seen the ghosts. But at the moment, spooks were the least of our problems.

As we reached the main staircase, there was something bugging me, but in my foggy state of mind I couldn't remember what it was. It just struck me that there was an important reason for us to get up to the second floor.

"Let's go up," I said.

"Are you sure that's a good idea, Frank?" Janet asked.

"That's where the guy that slugged me is." I started up the staircase. Janet was on my heels, her pistol held before her. Jo hesitated for a moment, then followed.

As we reached the top of the staircase, we could hear noises coming from the master bedroom suite. It sounded like the treasure hunters were trying to break through the plaster. For some reason this bothered me more than just the idea of the resulting physical damage.

It took them a moment to realize that we were watching them from the doorway. I turned the lights on with one of those old fashioned push-button switches. There were two of them, one tall and thin, the other of medium height. They were dressed as if for a costume party in somebody's idea of a twenties' gangster. I guess the idea was that if anyone spotted them they'd think they were the ghosts. As they turned to face us there was a look of surprise on their faces. Jo will do that to you if you aren't expecting her.

They had been trying to break through the plaster lath next to the fireplace, and each of them had a long pry bar in their hands which they waved menacingly.

"I wouldn't do that if I were you," I said with more bravado than I felt.

They moved closer to us. "You might have a gun, mister, but do you really think you and those two bimbo's you're with can take us?"

No one was expecting what happened next. Jo stepped forward with a left hook and followed it up with a right upper cut. The guy dropped like a rock.

"I don't mind being called a dame, or even a broad, but I sure ain't no bimbo, buster."

The guy still standing was debating how to react. I helped him along. "I'd drop it if I were you. My aim might not be so good at the moment, but Janet here can put one right between your eyes. I've seen her do it."

He must have agreed with me, because he let the pry bar fall from his hands.

"Jo, see if you can find something to tie him up with until the cops get here."

The was a drapery pull that seemed stout enough. Jo tied his hands behind his back, pulling the rope really tight. The intruder didn't resist. With a shove to the chest she pushed him down on the bed.

"And don't get up, buster, until I tell you to."

"Jo, why don't you keep an eye out the front window for the cops. They should be getting here soon, storm or no storm."

"Sure thing, Frank. Say, what were these two bums doing here, anyway?"

"They were looking for Fat Augie's treasure."

"But I thought that was supposed to be buried in the cellar."

"That's what everybody has thought. That's why no one has ever managed to find it."

It was coming back to me, the idea that had come to me that afternoon. I explained, "Everybody assumed that Fat Augie had a million bucks in gold coins hidden somewhere in the house. Well, a million bucks in coins, even gold ones, takes up a lot of room. The cellar would be the only logical place to stash it. But if you think about it, a million bucks in coins wouldn't have been of any use to Augie. He'd have wanted something portable that he could grab and stuff in a suitcase if he had to go on the lam. Something like bearer bonds. A stack of those worth a million would only have to be so high," I said, indicating a stack a few inches high with my thumb and forefinger.

"What these two yokels were looking for was a concealed safe. But they were looking in the wrong place."

"How do you know that, Frank?"

"Because I figured it out this afternoon, that's how. Take a look at where the turret joins the main house. If you look at the outside and inside walls you'll see that there's a dead space between that's maybe two or three feet wide. That's where Augie hid his safe. I just didn't have time to look for it this afternoon."

Jo eyed the paneling at the joint with a new appreciation. She started running her hands over the molding looking for a hidden catch. Janet went over to help her. Even the guy on the bed looked on with curiosity.

"I can't find anything, Frank."

"It's probably pretty well hidden. The release might not even be someplace close to the panel. It might be around the corner. We'll probably have to come in and pry the paneling off. It seems a shame, it's nice work. They don't make it like that anymore."

"For a million bucks I could care less about the workmanship, Frank," Jo said. "Just give me that pry bar."

"Maybe you won't have to bother," Janet said. Suddenly there was a click and one of the panels on the passageway between the bedroom and the turret popped open. Jo swung it wide on its hinges. Inside, we could see the door to a safe. It was an old-fashioned one, one worked by a key, not a combination dial.

"So what now, Frank? Dynamite?"

"Maybe not. Try one of these." I tossed her the ring with the keys to the house. There were about half a dozen keys on the ring besides the one that opened the front and back doors.

"Yeah. There was one I never could figure out what it went to."

Jo inserted the key in the keyhole and gave it a twist. It was stiff with a half century of disuse, but finally there was a snick as the lock freed. She gave the handle a twist and the door swung open.

"There sure isn't any gold, Frank, but there are some papers. Some kind of certificates."

Jo started to pull them out and examine them. "They're stock certificates, but to companies I've never heard of. Do recognize any of them, Janet?"

She handed the packet of stocks to Janet who examined them closely.

"When did Fat Augie die, Frank? It was before the big crash, wasn't it?"

"Yeah."

"Most of these stocks are gold mining shares. Real speculative stuff. Augie must have been like everyone else at that time and been playing the stock market in a big way. I'd be surprised if any of these are worth a thing today."

"Just my luck," Jo said.

"Don't feel too bad, Jo. At least when the story gets out, you won't have to worry about any more treasure hunters trying to break in."

"But what good is that going to do me? I've still got ghosts. I'll never be able to sell this place."

"One thing at a time, Jo," I said. My head was giving me troubles and all I wanted to do was sit down somewhere quiet.

The patrol car showed up soon after that. Janet went down to let them in through the front door. They weren't too sure what to make of Jo. She has that effect on people.

"She's the owner, officer," I explained. "You can check with Lt. Flannigan if you've got any questions."

"I guess that won't be necessary," one of the patrolmen responded. "These two have had run-ins with the law before. Mostly minor stuff. But they've done it now by slugging you from behind. I'm surprised that you were able to deck one in the shape you're in."

"Oh, that wasn't me. Jo did that. She took exception to being called a bimbo."

The cops looked at Jo with new respect. "That's mighty impressive, ma'am. Well, I guess we'll take these two down to the station. Things have been so busy with the storm tonight that they probably won't do anything more than toss them into a holding cell overnight. One of the detectives will probably be in contact with you in the morning to take statements and decide about charges."

One of the patrol officers got handcuffs on the two suspects and then took down our names and phone numbers. By this time, the intruder that Jo had knocked out was starting to come round and they were able to get the two down the stairs to the front hall.

"Are you sure you don't want us to call an ambulance for you?" one of the cops asked at the front door. "These head wounds can be tricky."

"No, I'll be fine," I assured him. I wasn't convinced of the fact. "But thanks anyway."

"We'd better get going, then. The night isn't half over."

We watched them escort their prisoners down the front walk to the waiting squad car. By then the storm had passed and there was only a thin drizzle remaining.

After the police drove off Janet shut the front door.

"I don't know about you, but I feel like calling it a night," Janet said.

"But what about the ghosts?" Jo asked.

"I think the ghosts can wait for another night," Janet replied. "I should get Frank to bed. He might be hard-headed, but he took quite a jolt."

"I guess you're right," Jo responded. "It has been a long night."

"Someone should go down and secure the latch on the scullery window. Turn out the lights, too," I said, not that I was volunteering.

"I'll do it," Jo said. "You'd better stay here with Frank."

While Jo was gone, I sank into a seat in the front hall at the foot of the staircase. Things were coming back into focus more. I remembered something that Janet had said when they had found me down in the cellar.

"Did you really see a ghost, Janet?"

She hesitated for a moment. "I think so, Frank. We saw something. I'm sure it wasn't those two that the police took away. Their builds were different and they were wearing different clothes. Of course, they were glowing and we could see through them, too. They certainly looked like ghosts."

"Why don't you tell me exactly what happened. I'd like to hear it from you before Jo gets back. She tends to be a bit imaginative at times."

Janet gave me one of her melt butter smiles.

"After you left to check the noise, we were sitting in the music room. The door to the hall was open. We had blown out the candles, so that we were sitting in the dark.

"It must have been ten minutes after you left that we saw them. They were walking slowly down the hall. There were two of them, both dressed in old-fashioned suits, just like you see in pictures from the twenties. You know, wide spaced pin-stripes, vests, dark-shirts, two-toned shoes. They were both wearing wide brimmed hats, too."

"You said they were glowing?"

"That's the strange part. Except for the lighting flashes, it was pitch dark in the hall, but I could see them clearly, make out all the details of how they were dressed. It wasn't at all like they had been painted in some sort of phosphorescent paint. They just kind of shown in a sort of monochromatic light. And Jo was right about another thing. I could see through them. I could make out the lines of the wainscoting in the hallway right through their bodies."

"I don't know what to say, Janet. What you're describing sounds like the classic description of a ghost. But ghosts don't exist."

"Don't they? Are you sure, Frank?"

"I thought I was."

"So what do we do now?"

"About what?" I asked a little densely.

"The ghosts, Frank. We can't just leave it like this. It wouldn't be fair to Jo, for one thing."

"What wouldn't be fair to Jo?" Jo asked. She'd come back from the basement and had obviously overheard the last bit of our conversation.

"It wouldn't be fair to you to leave you without doing something about the ghosts," Janet answered.

"I appreciate that, Janet, but I'm starting to think that Frank is right. This isn't something for us to handle by ourselves. This is something where we need professional help."

"Are you thinking about a priest, Jo?" I asked.

"Lord, no. I'm talking about a ghostbuster. Maybe if I get in touch with the Professor he'll be able to recommend someone."

Janet and I just stared at Jo. There are times when she just lives in another world.

"Well, we can't do anything more about it tonight and you had best get Frank home and tucked into bed. Just let me turn off the lights upstairs and then we can leave."

Neither of us objected. Jo ran up the stairs and was back in a few seconds leaving the upper floor in darkness.

"Ready? I'll just turn out the hall lights and we can leave."

Janet had the front door open. Jo hit the switch for the hall lights as I was getting up from where I had been sitting. When the lights went out, the only illumination was what was coming from the streetlights through the open door. That's when I saw them. The ghosts.

They looked just the way that Janet had depicted them, two guys dressed like twenties gangsters, except they were glowing with this pale light and you could see things through them. They were standing there holding a silent conversation. You could see their lips move, but there wasn't any sound. They seemed to be trying to decide what to do next.

I looked at Jo and Janet. I could tell they saw them, too. That made me feel better. I think.

The two ghosts seemed to have reached an agreement, for they turned and started to walk towards the back of the house.

Now if I'd been in a rational frame of mind I would have walked out the front door and dragged the girls with me. That certainly would have been the smart thing to do. Instead, I found myself starting to follow them towards the back of the house. It was only after I had taken a half-dozen steps that I noticed that Jo and Janet were following along behind me.

By this time the ghosts had reached the back stairs and started to descend to the ground floor. I looked at Jo and she nodded, so we followed. Janet had the flashlight in her hand and had turned it on so that it was pointing at the floor. We could still see the ghosts this way, but could make our way through the darkened house.

When we reached the foot of the stairs the ghosts had disappeared, but we could see a glow coming from the door to the cellar steps. We'd come that far, I guess we all felt there was no turning back. Down the steps we followed.

The ghosts were making their way towards the back of the house where the coal bunkers had been. They stopped at the edge of the bin. Again, they seemed to engage in a discussion, one of the ghosts waving his hands around as if emphasizing a point. The other one nodded in agreement. The two stepped into the coal bin and they vanished—

Just like that they were gone. Janet came up and splashed the beam of the flashlight around, but there was nothing.

"Jo, go back and turn on the lights. The switch is at the head of the stairs."

A few seconds later the cellar lights were on including a bare bulb just above our heads.

"You two saw them, didn't you?" Jo asked when she came back. "They were right here, and then they vanished."

"We saw it, Jo. The same thing you did."

"What happened?"

"I don't know. Maybe they went back to wherever ghosts go when they aren't busy haunting."

"Frank," Janet spoke up. "You said that Fat Augie killed them and buried them in the basement, didn't you?"

"That's what all the stories said. But they said there was a hoard of gold coins buried in the cellar, too."

"But what if it's true?" Janet asked. "What if Fat Augie did catch them? What if he did kill them, and buried them underneath the coal bin to dispose of the bodies? That would mean that this is their grave. Where else would a ghost go between hauntings?"

"That makes sense, Janet," Jo said. "Just like in all the ghost stories. That explains it. No wonder they haunt this place. I'd be mad, too, if I was buried in a coal bin."

"What do you think, Frank?" Janet asked.

"What do I think? Remember, I don't even believe in ghosts. But I'm thinking we talk to Flannigan, see if the cops want to dig up the coal bins. After all, technically it is still an open case, and there's no statute of limitation on murder. But that can wait until morning. I'm all for getting out of here and going to bed."

There weren't any disagreements.

It took a few days to work through the red tape and convince the authorities to excavate the coal bins. Jo didn't want any part of the dirty work. Neither did Janet, for that matter, so I ended up being deputized as Jo's representative.

It didn't take long once they started digging to find the first signs of a corpse. Fat Augie hadn't bothered to bury them deep, planning to dump a load of coal on top of the graves. After the first bones were found we had to wait for the M.E. to show up. It was slow going as they took a bunch of pictures to record every step of the disinterment. It took another four hours before the last bit of remains had been recovered.

There had been two of them, just as all the rumors had claimed. It had been damp in the cellar, and not much of their clothing remained, but from what was recovered, they had been dressed in rather flashy period suits just as the ghosts had been. They also found a couple of .45 slugs that the expert said probably came from a Thompson sub-machine gun. Fat Augie hadn't messed around. Perhaps it was fitting that he met his own end a few weeks later from a Tommy-gun burst.

The D.A. went through the motions of an inquest, but with a case that old, it wasn't surprising that the ruling was quickly decided to be willful murder, probably by Augustus Wenzel. As he was long dead, there was no point going further. Some papers were filed and the case was marked closed.

The remains of the two victims were buried. It wasn't much of a funeral. Two boxes of assorted bones were planted in the earth. A priest said a few words and then left. The only other people in attendance were Jo, Janet, and myself.

Funny thing is, though, Jo's haunted house problems ended when the bodies were dug up. No more apparitions in the night, no more spooks or weird noises. Word got out that the house was no longer haunted. As a piece of real estate it was still a white elephant, but the stigma was gone.

Finally, some foundation made an offer. They wanted to turn the place into a museum of something. The offer was probably for a fraction of what the place was worth, but it was still a lot of money to Jo. At least she wouldn't have to worry about retirement, and she was just glad to get it off her hands.

There was another funny thing. It was about those gold mining certificates that Fat Augie had planned to use for his get-away money. As Janet had guessed, most of them had proved to be completely worthless. Jo sold them to an antique dealer for a quarter each. They netted thirty-two dollars and fifty cents. But there was one that it turned out wasn't completely worthless. Just before the stock market crash the company that had issued it had been bought up by one of the West Coast oil companies. The deal had involved an exchange of stock. When Jo's lawyer had finally worked through all the stock splits, exchanges and mergers in the ensuing sixty or so years, it ended up with Jo making more on the stock than she cleared on the house. So Fat Augie had really hidden a treasure after all.

Jo still sings at the Blue Angel, but she takes Thursday nights off. They never do good business that night, anyhow.

As for me, do I believe in ghosts now? I have to say, I'm still not sure. My noggin had taken a pretty hard knock that night. Most of my memories after I got hit are a little fuzzy. I know what Jo and Janet say, and I'm not calling them liars, but I'm just not convinced. Maybe there is a rational explanation for what happened that night. Maybe. I can only hope.

The Fictional Detective Takes on Lady Luck

The Fictional Detective Takes on Lady Luck

It was Tuesday afternoon and I was in a bar shirking my responsibilities with rye on the rocks and a bit of soda water. Not that my responsibilities really amounted to much. I had a publisher who was clamoring for the first few chapters or at least an outline of *Death Buys a Condo*, a book for which I had to admit they had paid a reasonably generous advance. I had a first chapter and even part of the second, but I was damned if I had any idea of where the thing was going to go from there.

The bar's name was Lou's, but the neon sign out front just said "cocktails" and ended in a flourish that was the outline of a martini glass. It didn't really matter; the guy that owned the joint was named Ed. If there ever had been a Lou, he, or possibly she, was lost in the recesses of saloon history. Not that it was a saloon. It wasn't a beer joint, either. It was a dim bar where the patrons mostly drank hard liquor, though after five when the office crowd stumbled in, there was a tendency to add fruit and vegetables to the mix.

It was too early for that, and Ed, who was tending bar, and I had the place to ourselves except for one other guy who sat nursing a gin and tonic at the other end. He was a middle-aged guy, about medium height, skinny with the kind of pale skin that comes from not getting enough sun or eating enough vegetables. He had thinning brown hair and wore a rumpled suit that had seen better days.

I didn't really know him, but I knew that his name was Charlie. I think his last name was Johnson, but I could be wrong. Mostly people called him "Charlie Luck" if they called him anything at all. That was because he played the ponies. He bet on sporting events, too, and played slot machines when he could find them. He didn't play poker or roll dice or anything that required too much active participation. He wasn't called him Charlie Luck because he won. Far from it. As the song goes, *"If it weren't for bad luck, he'd have no luck at all."* That pretty much summed up Charlie. He won just often enough to keep the bookies and loan-sharks away. I don't know if he had a real job. If he did, it allowed him free time to spend drinking gin and tonics in the middle of the afternoon while he waited for the results to come in from the race tracks.

I'd been studying Charlie for a couple of minutes because there wasn't much else to do. That was my mistake, because I caught his eye. Charlie raised his glass in a salute, and I realized that he wanted to "talk." Part of what I like about bars like Lou's is that you can just sit there quietly and drink with no pressure to be sociable, but I had blown that and I realized I would have to indulge in conversation at least until I finished my drink.

Charlie slid his gin and tonic along the length of the bar and took the seat next to me.

"How's it going, Frank?" he asked.

"Oh, not too bad," I replied in a non-committal sort of way.

"Working on a new book?"

"Not at the moment. I'm drinking rye on the rocks. How are the ponies treating you these days?" I asked to deflect attention away from me.

"I can't complain." Usually, when someone says that they are about to do just that. Charlie was no exception, except that his complaint had a twist. "I've been winning pretty regular the last couple of weeks." Surprisingly, he didn't sound too happy about the fact.

"Well, here's to Lady Luck," I said, clicking my rye against his gin.

"I've never had a winning streak like this before, Frank," he said nervously.

"Oh?" I wasn't really that interested, but I thought I might pick up something I could use in a story.

"I haven't lost a bet I've placed in the last three weeks. Not one. It ain't natural, Frank. I keep expecting the other shoe to drop."

He was mixing his metaphors, but I didn't object, despite the fact that now that I was an author, or at least a writer, I had some grounds to do so. I could see that his situation was really bothering him. I couldn't see why, but I was actually starting to feel sorry for the guy.

"You could always stop gambling," I suggested.

"Oh, I couldn't do that," Charlie responded. I hadn't really expected anything else. "That would be, well, wrong. It's like I've been given this gift. The gift of luck. You don't turn your back on something like that, not if you don't want something bad to happen."

Still being new to the writing game, I wasn't sure whether that was a double or triple negative, but his logic was starting to get to me. "Let me get this straight. You are worried that if you keep winning, something bad will happen to balance things out. But if you stop gambling, something bad will happen because you're turning your back on your luck. Does that about sum it up?"

"Yeah, that's it exactly, Frank. I knew you'd understand."

I didn't understand at all. But I have to admit, I was intrigued. My glass was empty. Normally, I limit myself to one drink when I'm shirking my responsibilities, but I had the feeling I was onto something, so I ordered another and offered to buy Charlie one, as well.

"No, Frank. I'll buy. After all, I'm winning."

Ed came over to take our orders. Charlie reached into his pocket and pulled out a roll that would have choked the proverbial horse. He peeled off a twenty and laid it on the bar. Ed picked up the bill and looked at it real close like he expected it to be counterfeit before slipping it into the till.

"Thanks, Charlie," I said.

"So what do you think I should do, Frank?"

"About what?"

"About my luck. That's what we're talking about."

"Well, you could just keep riding it as long as it holds out. It's bound to break eventually, isn't it? I mean, winning streaks always end. They wouldn't be streaks if they didn't, after all."

"Yeah, I guess I'll have to," Charlie said with resignation.

"So how much have you won so far?" I asked, trying to edge away from a topic that was turning morbid.

"I don't know. Eighteen, nineteen grand, I guess. Maybe a little more after today."

I whistled. I'd never thought of Charlie as a high roller. He'd never had that much money, and he wasn't the kind of guy that would drop everything he had on a hunch unless he was down to just two dollars. From what I knew of him most of his bets were small ones, five bucks here, ten there. Unless he'd hit a real long shot it was hard to see how he could have made that much money.

"The bookies must be loving you."

"To tell the truth, they ain't been so happy to see me the last couple of weeks." At nearly twenty grand in losses, I bet they weren't.

There was a moment of silence while neither of us had anything to say.

"This is really bothering you, isn't it, Charlie?"

"Yeah, Frank. It is. I know I should be happy, but I'm not. I just wish things could go back to the way they were."

"You sure about that?" I asked.

"Kind of," Charlie answered seriously.

"Well, maybe what you need is to do something to break the spell."

"What do you mean, Frank?" Charlie looked puzzled but interested.

"Well, luck has got to have limits. It's like the conservation of energy or the second law of thermodynamics." I don't know much about either, but then I don't know that much about luck either. Mostly I was just spouting off the way guys who drink in bars in the afternoon do.

"I'm not sure I follow you, Frank?" Actually, I wasn't too sure of what I had meant myself.

"Let's just say there's only so much luck to go around. Now if you really want to break this winning streak, what you've got to do is place a bet that's so outrageous that it uses up all the luck in the streak. Place a bet, say, on a plodder that has never even placed let alone win."

"But I tried that, Frank. I put a bet to win on a horse named 'No Show.' He was sixty-seven to one."

"What happened?"

"The front runners got tangled up and fell. In the confusion No Show came in first. It paid sixty-seven fifty."

"That's pretty impressive. How much did you bet."

"Two bucks. I'm not crazy, Frank."

"But that's your problem, Charlie. So you win a little over a C-note. That's chump change. What you really need to do is place a really big bet on a long shot. Something that will really pay out. Something that matters. Something that will really use up a lot of luck."

"I guess I get you, Frank. It's not just the winning that uses up luck, it's how much is on the line."

"Yeah. It's all about the math. Big bet, more luck."

"You're right, Frank. I'll do it." Charlie actually seemed happy, like a big weight had been lifted off his shoulders. I was starting to feel a little guilty, because I hadn't really been taking the whole thing seriously.

"Now you need to think about this, Charlie. I wouldn't get carried away. Maybe you should put some of your winnings away for a rainy day. For your retirement."

"But, Frank," Charlie protested," I can't go on like this. I need to do something, and what you've suggested makes more sense than anything else I've thought of."

"No it doesn't, Charlie. I'm just a guy in a bar spouting off after a couple of drinks."

"Don't underestimate yourself. You're a genius, Frank. Thanks for the advice. I've got to get going, though. See you around."

Charlie finished off his gin and tonic, left a five dollar tip on the bar and walked out before I could stop him, leaving me staring at my reflection in the mirror behind the bar.

I shrugged. It wasn't my choice to make. Even if I did believe in Luck with a capital "L" which I didn't. I was tempted to have another drink, but I didn't. That might have been my second mistake, because as things unraveled over the next few weeks, I certainly could have used it.

It was several days later, Friday, in fact, that I next had contact with Charlie. It was the middle of the afternoon and

I was in my office working on *Death Buys a Condo*. Some of Charlie's luck must have rubbed off on me, because I'd polished off four more chapters and was deep in the middle of a fifth, writing the sex scene.

There's an unwritten law that every hard-boiled detective novel has to have at least one steamy sex scene in it, preferably involving the detective and the woman who will eventually be revealed to be the murderer. I was finding writing this one to be difficult. It's not that I have anything against sex, mind you, but I find writing about it, well, embarrassing, and this one was proving tough going.

That's why I wasn't particularly happy when I heard someone knocking on the frosted glass of the office door. I tried to ignore it, hoping they'd go away and leave me to write my sex bit in peace, but they were persistent. After a minute of rapping they were starting to sound desperate.

"Frank, I know you're in there." I recognized the voice as that of Charlie Luck. It didn't sound like he was going to go away any time soon, either.

I realized it was futile trying to work with him out there, so I got up and went to the door. When I opened it to tell him I was busy he shoved past me.

"Frank. I'm in trouble. You've got to help me."

"Look, Charlie. I don't do that kind of thing anymore. I'm a writer. It says so on the door." I pointed at the frosted glass where the "Private Detective" had been scraped off and replaced by "Writer." I thought that that had been a class touch at the time, but no one seems to pay any attention to the change.

I had been a detective. At least I thought I had been, though my memories of the past are a bit vague. I know that I still had a photo ID in my wallet certifying that I was a "Private Investigator" duly license by the state. I remember clearly that I had solved the murder of the famous mystery writer Ezekial O. Handler. Before that, not so much. That used to worry me, but I gave it up. Life was too good. I was married to a woman named Janet who not only was beautiful and could cook, but who had saved my life with a shot from .45 Colt automatic. It had been Janet who had convinced me to give up being a private dick and become a writer, instead. She had even used contacts she had made as Handler's mistress to wangle a contract with a publisher for three detective novels written by yours truly, Frank Slade.

"But you've got to help me, Frank. After all, it's all your fault," Charlie insisted.

"My fault? How'd you figure that."

"I did what you said."

"What? When?" I admit that Charlie had me a little confused seeing as I hardly even knew the guy.

"In the bar. On Tuesday. Don't you remember?"

"I remember having a couple of ryes on the rocks and talking to you about your winning streak."

"And you said that if I wanted to break it, I should use up all my luck by betting a bundle on a sure fire loser. Well that's what I did. I bet five grand on a nag that should have been sent to the glue factory years ago. Five grand to win."

"Look, Charlie. I'm sorry about the five grand, but you shouldn't take advice from anyone who's drinking alone in the middle of the afternoon. It's just not smart. You can't blame me if you lost."

"But that's just it, Frank. I didn't lose. Somehow that nag managed to come in first. The odds on favorite came up lame, the horse in second threw its jockey, you don't even want to know what happened to the horse in third. It was a disaster. Except for the horse I'd bet on."

"You won. So what's the problem?"

"That's just it. I won. I was supposed to lose."

"So you made a bunch of cash. What were the odds? Ten to one?"

"That nag? They were thirty to one, Frank."

"OK. So you made, what, 150 grand? I still don't see what your beef with me is."

"Look, Frank. Five grand is a pretty big bet in this town. There aren't many bookies that will accept that kind of money. My regular book wouldn't even touch it. I had to place it with one of the big boys."

"Who?" I was starting to get an uneasy feeling in the pit of my stomach.

"Slim Arneson," Charlie answered like he was handing down sentence at his own trial. Not that I blamed him. Slim Arneson had come down from the twin cities a few years back and taken over most of the high stakes gambling in town. He had a pretty ruthless reputation backed up by a crowd of ugly Swede muscle. Definitely not the kind of guy you wanted to owe money to. Not if you wanted to keep walking.

"So I still don't see what your problem is, Charlie. It's not like *you* owe *him* money, is it? He's the one that owes you."

"That's just it. Arneson is into me for a hundred and fifty large. And he can't pay it. He doesn't have the cash on hand. He's tapped out. Broke. Worse, he thinks that somehow I rigged that race to win just to break him."

"Well, if you accept your 'luck' theory, he's right in a way, isn't he?" I contributed perhaps a little unhelpfully.

"But you told me to do it, Frank," Charlie protested.

"I made a theoretical suggestion, Charlie. Let's get that straight."

"I'm dead meat. What am I going to do, Frank?" Charlie seemed like he was on the edge of becoming unhinged.

"Look, it can't be that bad, Charlie. Maybe you can work out an arrangement with Arneson. Terms. Like he pays you back what he owes five grand a week."

"You don't understand, Frank. I've been trying to tell you. He's got two of his muscle looking for me, Sven and Olaf. They've got orders to kill me. Arneson figures if I'm dead, he won't have to pay out."

I didn't know Sven and Olaf personally, but the word had been going around town that Arneson had brought in some pretty tough cookies from St. Paul to do his collecting for him. No corpses had been linked to them—yet.

"Well, maybe you should cut your losses, Charlie, and take a powder. I hear Florida is nice this time of year."

"Arneson is connected, Frank. I don't think I can get far enough away."

"Sounds like you've got a real problem, Charlie. I sympathize with you, I really do, but what is it you expect me to do?"

"I don't know, Frank. But I figured that you being a private detective and all, you'd come up with something."

"Like I told you before, Charlie, I don't do that kind of thing anymore. I'm a writer now. See, I've got a typewriter and everything," I said pointing at the Underwood sitting on my desk.

Charlie looked at me, the hope gone from his eyes. "I understand, Frank. It's not your problem." He looked like he was ready to walk that last mile to the gas chamber. That's when he got to me.

"Look, Charlie, you got a place you can lie low for a couple of days while I look into this thing for you?"

"I got a niece over on the east side. She might put me up for a couple of days." I'd never really thought of Charlie ever having any family before.

"OK. You go there. Don't even go back to your room. Give me a call on Monday, and I'll let you know if I've worked anything out."

"Thanks, Frank. I knew you wouldn't let me down." He extended his hand. I gave it a shake and saw him to the door realizing that I didn't have a clue what to do next.

The visit from Charlie had broken my concentration and after he had left I discovered I no longer was in the mood to continue my work on the sex scene. In my rather short career as I writer, I've discovered that if you aren't in the mood for that sort of thing you might as well not bother.

Instead, because it was already late afternoon, I decided to go home where I knew that my wife Janet would be preparing dinner after which, any sex scenes would be of the real rather than literary kind.

Janet is the sort of woman one typically finds only between the covers of the more lurid class of hard-boiled detective novels, i.e. she is tall, blonde, shapely and lethal with a pistol at close range. She's also a great cook. Before his demise, she had been the mistress of Ezekial Handler, and it was Janet who had hired me to track down the man responsible for the writer's murder. She shares with me a vagueness about her memories of the past, and if one were to believe Handler's last letter, we are both creations of that author's imagination. Of course, no rational person could believe such an incredible claim.

Dinner was, as usual, excellent, tenderloin with a brandy cream sauce, green beans, and potatoes au gratin. This was accompanied by a good California cabernet. I'd never been one much for wine before I met Janet, but then I hadn't been one much for tenderloin with brandy cream sauce, either.

As we ate, Janet asked me how my day had gone. She's as interested in my progress with *Death Buys a Condo* as my publisher is, though her suggestions tend to be more helpful. I recounted my visit from Charlie.

"You *are* going to help him, aren't you, Frank?" she asked when I had finished.

"I'll certainly try, but I'm not too sure what I can do."

Janet thought about that for a moment. "Do you believe in Luck, Frank?"

"I certainly was lucky when you walked into my life, Janet."

"That's sweet, Frank, but that's not what I mean. Do you believe in Luck, I mean as a tangible thing, not just some random fluctuation of statistics?"

"I guess I've never really thought about it. It's not one of my areas of expertise. What do you know about it?" Besides the good looks, Janet is anything but a "dumb" blonde. She has a lot of time on her hands and takes advantage of it by reading, and not just cheap detective novels, either.

"Not much, I'm afraid. It's not a subject that's treated seriously very often."

"Too bad. I could use some expert advice." I didn't give much credence to this "Luck" as a thing idea, but I'd seen too many odd things to dismiss it completely.

Janet seemed to be taking my comment seriously, for she paused, her fork poised in mid-air with a piece of tenderloin dripping sauce on her plate. She usually is a very elegant eater.

"There is one person you might ask, Frank. The Professor."

By the Professor she meant Professor Longwell. Longwell is an ex-carney turned stage magician. As a magician he's mediocre at best, good with card and coin tricks, but not so much with the bigger illusions. In addition to his stage show he makes some money on the side telling fortunes and holding séances. Mostly, that's just a con, but there are times when it actually does seem as if he can talk with the dead. He claims he has no control over this talent, and when it happens he can't remember a bit of it. I'm skeptical about that kind of thing, but I've seen him in action with results that I can't explain.

I'd met Longwell on my last case as a P.I. just before I got married and quit the business. He'd acted as a channel to a businessman named DuVille who had been murdered. Oddly enough, the information he had imparted led to the arrest of those responsible for the murder. I won't say that the Professor really was in contact with the spirit world, but I knew enough not to discount it.

"Longwell? I'm not sure that he's back from the Catskills." The Professor's reward for solving the DuVille case was a summertime engagement at a Borscht Belt resort owned by a cousin of a man who had been killed by the same murderer. For a guy like the Professor that was a big deal.

"I was talking to Josephine the other day," Janet responded, "and she mentioned that the Professor was back in town and performing at the Blue Angel Tuesdays, Thursdays and Saturdays. You might get in touch with him there."

I found it a little frightening that Janet and Josephine LaTouche had become bosom buddies lately. They don't have much in common. Janet is all woman and Josephine, well Josephine, nee Joseph Jaworski, is a female impersonator who headlines at the Blue Angel. Still, Josephine did seem to share something of our all too mysterious past. She'd sung at our wedding, too.

"That's an idea," I said none too enthusiastically. "Want to come along?"

"No, I think I'll pass, Frank. I've got a book I've been wanting to read." Whatever closeness she shared with Josephine didn't extend to the rest of the patrons and performers at the Blue Angel.

The next evening after dinner, I paid a visit to the Blue Angel. I hadn't been there in a while, it's not really my cup of tea. The Blue Angel is an attempt to recreate the sort of decadent bohemian night club that supposedly flourished in Berlin between the end of the Great War and the rise of the Nazis. Unfortunately, the limited budget has resulted in a rather dingy establishment where female impersonators and occasional novelty acts such as the Professor's share the stage. The clientele are a mix of those attracted to that sort of thing and those more conventional sorts out for a night on the wild side. What they get mostly is some mediocre entertainment and cheap booze at expensive prices.

I'd first stumbled into the place searching for a clue in the Handler case. That had led me to Josephine LaTouche who had been a friend of the late writer in a platonic sort of way. A former ironworker, Jo was nearly six feet tall with a penchant for blonde wigs and thirties evening gowns. Jo actually has a remarkably good voice and the ability to sell period songs like "Lili Marlene." She's worked her way up, if that term can describe it, to a position as the Blue Angel's headliner.

The guy on the door recognized me and let me in without collecting the cover. It was still early, and more than half the tables were empty. I went to the bar and ordered something safe to drink, rye and soda on the rocks, avoiding the more creative cocktails on the menu which had a tendency to be blue or glow in the dark.

I saw Jo working the floor to check the house and schmoozing with a party of indeterminate gender that was occupying one of the prime tables. I caught her eye, and after a bit she wandered over to where I stood at the bar.

Jo greeted me with a "Where've you been, big boy?" In heels and wig, Jo tops me by about four inches.

"Janet's been keeping me on a short leash." Jo and I know each other well enough that the flirtation remains verbal.

"Wise girl. What brings you to this den of iniquity?"

"I was hoping to talk to the Professor about something. Is he around?"

"I think he's in his dressing room. Want I should send him out?"

"When you get a chance."

"I've got to go back stage anyway to get ready. This glamour doesn't happen all by itself. Nice seeing you, Frank."

Jo wandered off, stopping to chat with a few of the regulars, before heading back stage. A little while later the Professor popped up next to me.

"Jo said you wanted to talk?" the Professor said as he took the stool and motioned to the bartender. The latter nodded and returned a few seconds later with a club soda on ice. The Professor doesn't drink when he's working, either for stage shows or the séances.

"Yeah. I need some technical advice. Why don't we grab a table?" A few moments later we were sitting at a table towards the back of the room where it was as quiet as it gets.

Professor Longwell is a thin guy slightly under medium height. He's pushing sixty and dresses conservatively when not on stage except for a Van Dyke beard and neatly trimmed curling moustaches. He ran away from an abusive home as a kid and joined a carnival which is where he picked up the magic trade, first as a shill and assistant, then as the act. He's best at the small stuff like cards and coins and is pretty consistent at things like mind reading. Somewhere along the line he discovered that he has a genuine if sporadic ability as a medium, or at least so he claims. I've seen him at work and haven't been able to figure out the dodge if there is one.

"So, what's the deal, Frank? You didn't come down here just to find out how to win at Three Card Monty."

"What do you know about Luck?"

"Luck? I've had bad luck and good luck and no luck at all. Luck is fleeting, luck is fickle. According to Sinatra, Luck is a Lady tonight." What more is there to know? But I sense that that's not what you want to hear, is it?"

"No. I'm talking about Luck with a capital 'L'. I ran into this guy. He's a small time gambler. Bet's the ponies, football games, that kind of stuff. No poker or dice or anything. He wins, he loses, but mostly loses. About three, four weeks ago he starts to win consistently. All the time. He can't even lose when he tries. He's put a bets on a some real long shots and won."

"Sounds, well, lucky," the Professor commented. "So what's the interest?"

"This guy has got himself in a jam. We were talking in a bar the other afternoon and I gave him some flip advice. He took it."

"And he lost some money and is now sore at you?"

"No, that's just it. He took my advice and bet a bundle on a refugee from the glue factory. He won. Something like a hundred and fifty grand."

"And this is your problem how? Seems like the guy should be thanking you."

"It's like this. The guy placed a bet with a bookie who's got a reputation for rough stuff. Worse, the bookie doesn't have the funds to cover the bet. Plus, he thinks the race might have been rigged somehow. He's not too happy with the situation and the word is out that he might be thinking that the easiest solution to his problem is to kill the guy I know."

"Yes, I can see how that might be a problem. There's no one more vindictive than someone crooked who thinks he's been conned. Just who is this bookie we're talking about?"

"Slim Arneson."

The Professor looked at the ceiling for a moment rolling his eyes. "I've heard about him, Frank. My best advice for your friend is to catch the next freight out of town and just keep going. But that's not what you want to hear, is it? Just what is it you want from me? Do you want me to put him in one of my boxes and make him vanish? It doesn't work that way, Frank."

"It comes back to my first question, Professor. Just what is Luck? Is there such a thing? And if there is, how do you get rid of it?"

"In my experience, there is no such thing as luck. People who win at cards win because they know what they're doing. People who win at dice—they're cheating. People who play the horses are just crazy."

I gave the Professor a look that said I wasn't buying it.

"You're serious, Frank, aren't you? I don't know if I can help you. Lots of things have been written about luck, but it's mostly hooey or statistics."

"But have you ever heard of someone suddenly getting so lucky that they *can't* lose?"

"Look, Frank. I've been around a long time. I worked carneys most of my life. I've heard all sorts of stories about luck, good and bad. Most of them are just that, stories. But there always have been rumors about guys who get real lucky for a while. It usually ends up bad, though."

"But how did they become lucky? And more importantly, how can you break the spell or whatever it is? This guy I know isn't greedy. This Luck thing has just brought him nothing but grief. The way he figures it, one of these days the universe is going to rebalance itself, and when it does things are going to go bad for him in a big way. And the longer he keeps winning, the bigger the fall is going to be."

"Karma."

"Yeah, something like that."

"He may be right. Particularly if Slim Arneson catches up with him."

"But is there anything that can be done about it?"

"About Arneson? That's more in your line, Frank, than mine. But as to the other? Well, this is what I know. Or at least it's what I've heard about or read about over the years. When someone suddenly becomes lucky it's usually because they've acquired some sort of talisman or magical object. Like a rabbit's foot, only a thousand times more powerful."

"Are there such things?"

"Who knows? I've never seen one that I thought was real. It's always you hear it from a guy who knew someone who was told this story about some guy in another town down the line. Do I believe it? Not really. But there are lots of things that I don't believe in that I've seen with my own two eyes."

"So, if I understand you, if the luck is coming from this talisman or whatever, all you have to do is get rid of it and the luck goes away and life returns to normal?"

"It usually doesn't work out so neatly. At least in the stories. Mostly what happens is that trying intentionally to get rid of the talisman brings down the wrath of the gods and the guy with the luck dies a horrible, painful death. That's probably not what your friend wants, is it?"

"Probably not. Of course if Arneson catches up with him, he might die a horrible, painful death anyway."

"You have a point," the Professor agreed sagely.

"So, any bright ideas?"

"No, but we're talking hypotheticals, anyway. We don't even know if there is a talisman involved?"

"What would it look like?"

"It could be anything, really. A coin, a trinket, a piece of clothing."

"Would you know one of these talismans if you saw it?"

"Do I look like a magician? Don't answer that, Frank. I know that I have a certain sensitivity to the supernatural, but I really can't say. I've never come across one of these things before. At least not a real one."

"Would you be willing to give it a try? Could you meet this guy on Monday, say in my office, if I could arrange it? The way this guy has been winning, I'm sure he'd be willing to pay a consultation fee."

"For you, Frank, and fifty bucks, I'll do anything."

"OK. I'll let you know."

"Well, I've got to get ready for my act." He slammed the rest of his club soda and got up.

After the Professor left for backstage, I hung around thinking about what he had said, but when the first act came on, I decided to split. Like I said, it's just not my thing.

Charlie called me on Monday, and we made arrangements to meet at my office that afternoon. I called the Professor and he agreed to be there. After that I got back to work on *Death Buys a Condo.*

I'd gotten to the chapter where the P.I. starts to suspect that the dame might be trying to double cross him. This is a crucial point in every hard-boiled detective story ever written. It has to be written with a lot of finesse for things to really work, and I was pretty engrossed in what I was putting down on paper. That's how I missed it when my visitors walked in.

I had just finished a paragraph and looked up to catch my breath when I noticed these two Vikings standing in front of my desk. By Vikings, I don't mean the whole horned helmet thing. These guys were dressed in suits that stretched tightly across their chests except for the bulges which I guessed were concealing shoulder holsters and guns. They were both six foot fourish, with blonde hair trimmed short. They might have passed for football players, but somehow I suspected neither had attended college. I was guessing that they were Sven and Olaf, Arneson's muscle.

"Where is he?" the one on the right asked. I wasn't sure if it was Sven or Olaf at that point, not that it matters.

"Where is who?" I retorted not too brightly.

"Charlie Luck."

"He's not here. Take a look for yourself." My office is about ten feet square and pretty much devoid of hiding places.

"Don't get wise, Slade." This was from the other one. Olaf or Sven. Take your pick.

"Look, fellas. I don't know where Charlie is." Strictly speaking this was true. I didn't see the need to mention that he was coming to see me in a couple of hours. "And in case the word hasn't gotten around, I'm not a P.I. anymore. I'm a writer. It says so on the door in case you can't read."

This seemed to have struck a nerve with the one on the left because he started to reach into his jacket for his gun. The other one stopped him with an outstretched hand, his cold, blue eyes boring into me at the same time.

"Mr. Arneson is looking for Charlie, Slade. Getting in his way wouldn't be smart. Mr. Arneson has ways of dealing with people who cross him. That's Sven and me." That answered my question as to which was which, not, as I said, that it mattered.

"I'll keep that in mind if I should run across Charlie. I'm sure that he'd be interested to know. Particularly as the word is out that Arneson is into him for a hundred fifty large."

That really struck a nerve. A bookie who gets a reputation for welshing on his bets doesn't stay a bookie long.

"Just remember, Slade. You've been warned." The Viking invasion withdrew as silently as they had come.

After they had gone, I reached into my desk for some Dutch courage, my hand shaking so badly I could hardly get the rye in the glass.

Charlie showed up just after one, looking worse than usual. He had that hunted sort of look in his eye. I can't say that I blamed him.

While we waited, I explained about the Professor. Charlie was dubious, but desperate enough to try anything. We didn't have long to wait.

"Shut the door and lock it, Professor," I said after he came in. "We don't want any unwanted visitors interrupting us." I went on to explain my encounter with the Viking twins. Charlie looked like a scared rabbit. The Professor just looked uncomfortable.

"I still don't understand why you wanted me to meet this guy, Frank," Charlie complained. "No offense intended."

"None taken," the Professor responded with the same smoothness he uses on hecklers at the Blue Angel.

"It's like this, Charlie," I started to explain. "You said that this Luck of yours was a sudden thing. You were going along normally, losing more than winning, then all of a sudden you can't lose to save your life. Literally, as it turns out. Well, the Professor is an expert of sorts on such matters, or at least as much of one as I could come up with. He's got some ideas about your situation, so why don't you hear him out."

"Whatever you say, Frank. I'm a desperate man."

"Thank you, Charlie. To begin with, you say this Luck of yours came on all of a sudden. Is that correct?"

"Yeah. One day I'm going along like normal picking maybe one winner out of half a dozen, and then the next day, I pick six in a row. All winners. All at good odds. Six five dollar bets and I'm up five hundred and fifty bucks. I haven't lost a bet since, even when I put my money on real stinkers."

"Did anything unusual happen between those two days?" the Professor interrogated.

"Like what? One day is pretty much like another for me unless the horses ain't running."

"Well, did you meet an unusual stranger?"

"Well I meet some pretty odd ducks playing the ponies, but I don't remember anybody that stands out."

"That's okay, Charlie. Did you acquire anything out of the ordinary?"

"Like what?"

"Oh, I don't know. A ring, a piece of jewelry, a token of some sort, a coin."

"No, nothing like that. Well—except maybe a coin."

"A coin, Charlie?" the Professor asked, suddenly attentive.

"Yeah, well, after the race results came in I was pretty much tapped, so I settled for a hot dog from this vendor for dinner. There was a funny coin in the change he gave back. I didn't notice it at first. Thought it was just a silver dollar, but when I took a look at it I thought there was something funny about it. I tried to go back and complain, but the vendor had moved."

"I see. And do you still have this coin?"

"Yeah. I've been afraid to pass it, cause it might be counterfeit."

"Could we see it?"

"Sure."

Charlie dug into his pocket, came up with a handful of change and extracted a coin. He held it in the palm of his hand, flipping it over so we could see both sides. When the Professor reached over to pick it up he clenched his fist as if he was reluctant to part with it.

Charlie had been right, the coin was about the size and shape of a silver dollar, but I doubt if it had ever come from any U.S. mint. It was well worn, and there were no signs of milling marks on the edge. The "heads" side bore the image of a seated woman in a long flowing robe, except it wasn't Lady Liberty. There was an inscription, too, "Buono Fortuna." The "tails" side had an image of a scale, like the scale of justice, except this one was tipped far to the right.

"I've never seen a coin like that before, Professor," I remarked.

"Nor have I, Frank. I'd judge it to be pure silver. The inscription is Italian, or maybe Latin. It means good fortune.

I presume that the woman is meant to represent the goddess of luck. Lady Luck, you'd call her."

"But it's not a real silver dollar, is it?" Charlie queried.

"No, Charlie. It certainly isn't. It might be a token coined by a casino someplace. They do sometimes make them for use on the premises. This looks a little too old for that, though. It might be from some gambling joint from the twenties or earlier," he said uncertainly.

"But you don't think so, do you, Professor?" I chimed in.

"No. You're right, Frank. I suspect that this coin is much, much older than that."

"How much older?"

"The medieval period, maybe even Roman times."

"You're saying that this coin is maybe two thousand years old and there's some hot dog vendor handing them out?"

"I doubt that the vendor knew what he had," the Professor explained. "I suspect that he got it from a customer, and recognizing that it wasn't legal tender, tried to pass it off on the first unsuspecting customer he could."

"But what about the Luck thing?" I countered.

"Maybe he didn't gamble? Maybe he just didn't associate the coin with his sudden good fortune."

"Look," Charlie interrupted. "I don't care how I got this thing, or how old it is. What you are saying is that it's responsible for my 'luck.' That means if I get rid of it, things will go back to being like they were. Is that right?"

"It may not be as easy as that, Charlie," the Professor cautioned.

"What do you mean?"

"The Lady Luck may not take kindly to being tossed aside. The consequences of such an act could be serious."

"More serious than having a mobster that wants to kill me?"

"I admit that your current situation is less than ideal—" the Professor started to say."

"Less than ideal?" Charlie interrupted. "You're not the one he's planning to give the cement overshoes to."

"Don't get excited, Charlie," I interposed. "The Professor is just saying that you have to be careful about what you do. Besides, are you sure you want to get rid of it. Except for the Arneson thing, you've been doing pretty well for yourself. Are you sure you want to go back to being a loser?"

"At least people weren't trying to kill me most of the time."

"Look, we don't even know if this coin has anything to do with your luck."

"I'm afraid we do, Frank," the Professor said seriously. "As you know, I sometimes can detect unusual auras around certain people of things. Well I sense such an aura around the coin, and Charlie, too. A very powerful aura unlike anything I've ever seen."

"Is this guy on the level, Frank?" Charlie asked, raising an eyebrow.

"Trust me on this one, Charlie. If anyone can detect auras, it's the Professor."

"Thank you for that vote of confidence, Frank," the Professor remarked sarcastically.

"So what do I do?" Charlie asked forlornly. "I can't get rid of this thing, and if I keep it, Arneson is going to kill me."

"What we need is a plan," I said.

Charlie and the Professor looked at me expectantly.

"I didn't say I had one," I clarified. "I said we needed one."

Tuesday morning came and I still didn't have a plan. I was having a case of writer's block on *Death Buys a Condo* too. All in all, my day wasn't going very well. It didn't improve any when a rapping sounded on my door. It sounded like a hard metal object was beating against the wood, not hard, but loud enough to be annoying. I tried to ignore it, but it persisted.

Finally, deciding that the only way to make it stop was to get up and tell it to go away, I went to the door and opened it. What I saw reminded me of a scene from one of those movies from the forties that had tried to cash in on the success of *The Maltese Falcon* but failed. I was confronted by two gentlemen, if that term could be so applied, dressed in the sort of linen suits that were fashionable in the tropics once upon a time. Considering the season, it was a poor choice. They were an ill matched pair, one short and stocky, the other tall and cadaverous looking. The stocky one was holding a walking stick with an ornate metal head, presumably the instrument that had been used to beat on my door.

"I'm not in the market for encyclopedias," I said. "Magazines, either."

"Ah, Mr. Slade. You *are* at home," the stocky one commented. He had a swarthy complexion and what hair he had left was black and oily. I couldn't place his accent. Let's just say he wasn't from around here.

"That depends," I responded in a surly tone. "Who's looking for him."

"Amusing, Mr. Slade. I am Horace Narcissian." He pronounced Horace so that it sounded like the Egyptian God. "My associate here is Mr. Thicke."

I couldn't think of a more ironic name. Thicke was six foot four if an inch and I doubted if he weighed more than a hundred fifty pounds. One side effect of his thinness was that I could see the bulge produced by a shoulder holster under his tropical suit.

"You seem to know who I am, so I'll skip the introductions."

This seemed to give Narcissian a momentary pause. After consideration he continued, "We would like to engage your services."

"Unless you want me to write a pulp novel, you're out of luck."

"You are a private investigator, are you not, Mr. Slade?"

"Take a look at the door. Notice that it says 'Writer.' I gave up the P.I. business some time ago. I didn't like some of the clientele."

"Still, Mr. Slade, I beg of you to hear me out. It will only take a moment of your time and it might well be to your benefit."

It was clear I wasn't going to get rid of these two oddballs easily, so I gave in.

"OK. You've got five minutes. Make your spiel." I resumed my seat behind the desk. I didn't offer my visitors a seat, but Narcissian took one anyway. Thicke continued to stand.

"I am, Mr. Slade, a sometime dealer in certain antiquities. I came to your fair city looking for a certain object. A coin in fact. In and of itself, it has no great intrinsic value, but it does have some historical interest."

"That's all very well, Mr. Narcissian, but I'm not a coin dealer."

"I am aware of the, Mr. Slade. If you will let me continue. I had made arrangements to procure this coin from a certain individual. Unfortunately, before we arrived, he met with a rather unfortunate accident, namely, he was run over by an automobile, and is now deceased."

"Sounds like you need to deal with his estate."

"Well, Mr. Slade. It appears that just before his demise, this individual, either intentionally or by accident passed the coin to a vendor of street food."

"Careless of him," I interrupted. "Odd that the vendor would have accepted it. They're usually pretty careful about money."

"The coin is much the same size and weight as an American silver dollar. It is quite possible that in the rush of business it might be mistaken for one."

"So this food cart guy has the coin. Why come to me?"

"By some odd quirk of fate, this individual also suffered an auto accident. When we approached his widow, we were able to determine that he no longer had the coin in his possession. Presumably he handed it out as change in some transaction."

"Sounds like you're out of luck, Mr. Narcissian. Though perhaps not as much out of luck as the last two people who had this coin in their hands. Are you sure you really want it?"

He looked surprised at the question. "Of course I want it, Mr. Slade," he said sharply. I've come a great distance to obtain that coin. It would be a shame to return empty handed. And to suggest that the coin had some part in the unfortunate fates of those two individuals is rank superstition. I'm surprised that a man of your intelligence would even suggest such a thing."

"I've rarely been accused of an excess of intelligence, Mr. Narcissian, but I'm afraid I still can't help you. Like the door says, I'm a writer now, not a P.I. Even if I were still in the business, I don't see as how there is much to go on. The food cart operator could have passed this coin on to any one of his customers."

Narcissian weighed this statement with great care. Finally he seemed to come to a decision. "Very well, Mr.

Slade. There is one piece of information that I have withheld up to this point. We have reason to believe that the person who has the coin goes by the name 'Charlie Luck.' Not, evidently, his real name, but one that he is well known by. We have tried to find him, but he has not been seen at any of his usual haunts since last week. You are familiar with this city, Mr. Slade. I am not. I would be willing to offer you, say, five hundred dollars if you could arrange an interview between this Charlie Luck and myself. Quite a sum for a task that should pose little risk to yourself."

"Five hundred dollars, eh? I thought you said this coin had no great intrinsic value?"

"Well, Mr. Slade. You will remember that it does have a certain historical interest. One that I may be able to capitalize on."

"I'll be honest with you, Mr. Narcissian. There was a time not so long ago that I would have jumped at such an opportunity. These days, though, I have all the money I need and little interest in wild goose chases."

"But Mr. Slade—"

"I've given you your five minutes, Mr. Narcissian. You've had your say. Now I'll have mine. I'm not interested. That's my final word on the subject."

"You're sure—"

"Yes!"

"Then my associate and I will cease to trouble you and bid you good day."

He stood ponderously and headed for the door with Thicke in his wake.

"Oh, Mr. Slade. If you should change your mind, here is my card. I am staying at the Excelsior Hotel."

I took the card and ushered the two out the door, locking it behind them.

Just what, I asked myself at the time, had Charlie gotten himself into? More importantly, how was I going to get him out of it. If Narcissian was to be believed, just passing the coin on to some other poor individual wasn't a solution, at least a satisfactory one. It seemed to have resulted in the death of the two previous owners of the coin.

At dinner that night I went over events with Janet. She didn't know Charlie at all, but there is something in her makeup that wants to back the underdog.

"You *do* have a plan, don't you, Frank?" she asked as she was cleaning up after dinner. It had been a pork schnitzel with peppers and onions served with fried potatoes. She'd found some decent Munich Oktoberfest to go with it, even though she isn't ordinarily a beer drinker. In our short married life, I'd learned that a meal like that meant she wanted me to do something.

"Not at the moment, baby," I replied.

"But you can't just leave Charlie dangling like that. You've got to do something for your friend."

"Janet. Charlie's not my friend. He's just some guy I met in a bar. We just talked over a couple of drinks."

"Frank! You've got to help him. This Narcissian man sounds dreadful." Janet usually isn't the whiny sort. Unless she's trying to annoy me, that is.

"It's Arneson that Charlie has to worry about."

"See."

"You were the one who wanted me to give up the detective business."

"But this is different."

"I could end up just as dead."

"That's not the way the Frank Slade I know thinks."

I know when to give in. "I don't have a plan yet, but I'm working on it."

"Are you really?"

"Sure."

"Do you want some desert?"

The next afternoon I got a call from the Professor asking if I was going to be around for a while. When I told him I was, he said that he'd stop by. He had something to tell me.

A half hour later I'd gotten the hero of *Death Buys a Condo* in a jam and was trying to figure a way to get him out of it, when a knock sounded on the door. Since Narcissian's visit I'd taken to locking it. When I asked who it was, the Professor answered.

"Getting a little nervous, Frank?" Longwell said as he eased his way in.

"No. I've just been having too many unplanned visitors." I gave him a quick synopsis of Narcissian's call the day before. He found the story interesting, but hadn't ever heard of Narcissian or Thicke.

"So what's up, Professor?"

"I may have some info on that coin of Charlie's"

"Oh?"

"Yeah. I know this guy. He's an amateur magician that comes around the club sometimes. He's not very good, but he knows it and doesn't really care. He's an okay guy. Buys me a drink after my act and we talk sometimes. It turns out he's a professor, a real one. Anthropology. At the U. Perhaps not coincidentally his area of interest is superstitions, mostly Southern European. Lingering influences of the old Roman and Greek gods and goddesses. That kind of thing."

"OK. So you know this anthropologist," I said

"Anyway, I went to see him yesterday. To talk about Luck and Fortune and good luck charms, that kind of thing. I didn't tell him about Charlie's coin. I told him I was looking for some stuff I could use as patter for an illusion I was working on based on Lady Luck. He seemed to buy into the idea. He became quite enthusiastic, in fact. We talked for a couple of hours."

"I hope this is leading somewhere," I interjected.

"Show some patience, Frank," the Professor responded. "He got off on the subject of the goddess Fortuna. It turns out the idea is really old. Pre-Roman, in fact, maybe Etruscan. Anyway, the Romans built a couple of temples to her, and the cult spread throughout the empire. She was appealed to for good luck generally and for good results in child-birth, that kind of thing. He went on about she became associated with the Egyptian goddess Isis and a bunch of other things like that. Now, like I said, the professor's area of research has to do with how some of the older ideas have carried over into modern times. He seemed to think that when people talk about 'Lady Luck' they are really drawing on the traditions surrounding Fortuna."

"Sounds reasonable." I could tell the Professor was getting worked up on the subject so I let him talk.

"Now this is where it gets interesting. The image of Fortuna often appeared on coins along with a cornucopia as the giver of prosperity. Sound familiar?"

"It sure does. But from what you've said, these coins used to be real common. Why does this particular coin seem to have some extra mojo?"

"Good question, Frank. I kind of let on that the premise of my illusion was going to be based on the power of some sort of magic talisman associated with Lady Luck, and I asked if he had any suggestions of background that I could use to feed the yokels. He got real interested then. Said he'd read a paper somewhere on the subject. He spent the next fifteen minutes rummaging around his office until he found it. It was by some German who'd uncovered a manuscript an eighteenth century monk had written. This monk had spent years collecting bits of folklore about Fortuna."

"It seems that there is a legend about a particular group of Fortuna worshippers that were also reputed to be powerful magicians. As part of their cult they conducted ceremonies to endow a special coin with the attributes of the goddess. Whether they did this with one coin or more isn't clear in the legends. Anyway, according to the legend this coin grants whoever possesses it success at any gaming event or wager."

"That certainly sounds like Charlie's coin."

"It does, doesn't it," the Professor agreed proudly.

"Now for the down side. This coin, according to the legend, while it grants success at gambling, doesn't extend to other aspects of the owner's life. It seems that the magicians who performed the rituals made a couple of mistakes along the way. The history of the coin is full of bad things happening to those that possess it. And obviously, lots of people were willing to use any means to gain possession of the coin."

"I can imagine," I said. "So did this paper make any mention of how to get rid of it."

"You have to understand, Frank, the paper was in German and my friend was sort of translating on the fly and he's not as good with German as he is with Latin or Italian, so I only got part of what it said. One thing was pretty clear, though. If the owner tries to give the coin away something really bad will happen to them. Of course, these old legend always have catches like that."

"There may be something to it in this case. From what this Narcissian character told me, the last two guys who had the coin before Charlie both died in accidents. The first guy was literally run over by a bus, after he had used it to pay for a hot dog. The hot dog vendor who gave it to Charlie as change was also killed in an accident shortly thereafter. Things aren't looking so good for Charlie. If he hangs on to it, chances are good that Arneson is going to have him killed, and if he gives it away he'll end up being run over or killed in some other gruesome way. Did this paper say there was any way out of this dilemma?"

"Not that my friend mentioned," the Professor said soberly.

I looked at him for a moment. Usually, the Professor is a pretty upbeat guy, which considering the life he's led is pretty remarkable. But he seemed very discouraged.

"So what do you think, Professor. Is that paper the real story, or is it a bunch of hooey?"

Longwell looked me in the eye. "You know, Frank, normally I take things like this with a grain of salt. But we've both seen things we can't really explain. I just don't know. But it doesn't look good for Charlie, does it?"

"No, it doesn't."

"What about Arneson? Have you come up with a plan for dealing with him, yet?"

"No, not yet. But I'm working on it. I'm working on it."

"That means you haven't got a clue, doesn't it?"

"That about sums it up."

I finally heard from Charlie on Friday night. How he'd gotten the number for the apartment I don't know. He was obviously agitated and it took a few moments to get him to calm down enough to tell me what the problem was.

"Somebody's following me, Frank."

"I thought you were going to lay low. Are you still at you're niece's?"

"Naw. She's a good kid, but after a few days we were getting on each other's nerves. I left a grand on the nightstand of the guest room and split. Besides, I didn't want to bring any of my trouble down on her."

Charlie might be a hopeless gambler, but at heart he's a decent guy.

"So where have you been staying?"

"I took a room in a boarding house off of Tyler Avenue. No one knows me there, but as long as I pay cash, they don't care."

"You haven't been flashing your bankroll around, have you, Charlie?"

"Give me some credit, Frank. I wasn't born yesterday. I keep just enough in my wallet to cover expenses. As far as the landlady knows, I'm an out of work salesman."

"So why do you think you're being followed?"

"Because since yesterday I keep running into the same guy. I went down to the pool hall on the corner to place a few bets on the ponies because there's this guy there who makes book. Nothing big, just five bucks a pop. I saw this other guy when I left the boarding house, just hanging around. When I came out of the pool hall he was standing across the street pretending to read a paper. He's hard to miss, though."

"What's he look like? Big guy? Swedish or Norskie or some such?" I asked, thinking of Sven and Olaf.

"Not that I can tell. He looks more like a zombie. He's real tall, skinny as a rail and pale as a ghost. It's freaking me out, Frank."

"Sounds like a guy named Thicke." I went on to tell him about Narcissian's visit. "Thicke carries a gun, Charlie, but I don't think he'll use it. It might be best, though, if you find a new place to stay."

"But I'm paid up till the end of the week."

"You can afford it, Charlie. What you can't afford is to end up dead. Remember that."

"OK, Frank. Whatever you say."

"And keep a low profile, this time. No betting."

"Sheesh. When are you going to get me out of this, Frank? I can't keep living like this. It's killing me."

"I'm working on it, Charlie. I'm working on it." Not that I had a clue what I was working on. "Give me a call when you find new digs."

Not much happened over the weekend. On Monday I actually got a full days' work in on *Death Buys a Condo*, by which I mean I wrote a couple of thousand words in the morning, had lunch and a beer, and then went back to the office and wrote another thousand words. The plot was coming along nicely and I was beginning to get an idea of how to end it.

I was in a pretty good mood when I knocked off around four-thirty, and maybe I wasn't paying as much attention as I should have been. There's a parking lot a block over from my office where I park my Chevy. I get a monthly rate, I don't have to worry about finding a place to park, and there's someone around during the day who sort of watches over things. It's not the best of neighborhoods, but usually you don't have to worry during the day.

I was halfway to the lot when I realized that I was being followed. I looked back and recognized my tail as Sven. Or maybe Olaf. I was so distracted that when I turned back around I ran straight into the chest of Olaf. Or maybe it was Sven. I guess big Swedes all look alike.

I tried to back away, but I was pretty much sandwiched between the two of them. The one behind me grabbed me by the arms, pinning them to my sides.

"We've been looking for you, Slade," Sven said.

"Well, it looks like you found me, boys. Is Arneson ready to pay his debts?"

"Don't get smart with us, dick. Where's Charlie?"

"How should I know?"

"Do we have to get rough?"

I looked around. The street was deserted. There were no signs of the cavalry coming to my rescue.

If there was one thing I had learned as a P.I. was that a lot of times it's better to use your brains than your muscle. This is particularly true when confronted by two guys who combined make three of you. I could tough it out, but that would probably result in a beating. With luck I'd just end up puking my guts out, but I might also end up in the hospital or worse. Or I could think of something clever to tell them. I chose the latter.

"OK, OK. There's no need for violence. Charlie's staying at the Excelsior Hotel. He's using a fake name. The room is registered under the name of Narcissian. He might have a friend with him for protection. Tall, skinny guy goes by the handle of Thicke."

"Think he's telling the truth, Olaf?" Sven asked.

"He's too stupid to lie," Olaf replied. I could have taken offense at that remark, but it didn't seem the time or place.

"He'd better not be, or we'll have to come back and finish things," Sven commented.

Olaf let go of my arms, and the two walked off as if nothing had happened. I dusted off my pride and headed for the car. I was under no illusion that that would be the end of things, but with luck, Thicke might plug one of the Viking twins before they got a chance to wipe the floor with him. Whichever way it went, I figured that I had solved at least one of my problems and bought some time for Charlie.

At the time, I didn't realize how prophetic my thoughts would be. I went home to the apartment where Janet had cooked a nice dinner, and tried to put the whole business out of my mind. Of course, that didn't prevent reality from rolling on to intrude later when it was most inconvenient.

I was working on the ending of *Death Buys a Condo*, the part where the hero confronts the villain and resolves the whole matter in a hail of bullets and a flurry of uppercuts. Endings are always tricky to write. Put in too much action and it seems like padding, but if you don't have enough the reader lifts his head from the story wondering what he has missed. In their own way, endings are as hard to write as the sex scenes.

I wasn't pleased then when a knock sounded at my door. It was an authoritative rapping, but not an impatient one. There was only one person that I knew capable of that kind of knock—Lt. Flannigan, one of the city's finest.

Flannigan and I have a sort of love/hate relationship that goes back as far as either one of us can remember, which frankly isn't all that far back. In my moments of deepest introspection I'm inclined to think that Flannigan is another product of Handler's imagination, a creature of his typewriter and a certain amount of magical mojo. Most of the time I just think he's a cop. We tolerate each other. We've even been known to cooperate. He was best man at my wedding.

Bowing to the inevitable, I got up and opened the door. Flannigan was standing there patiently, his fedora pushed back on his head, his rumpled suit laying carelessly on sagging shoulders. He looked for all the world like a caricature of a hard-guy cop from some 1950's detective story, a pose which I suspect is intentional.

"Hi, Frank." Flannigan isn't long on prose.

"Pat," I responded, recognizing that our conversation was falling into a clichéd pattern that would have been familiar to any fan of the hard-boiled genre.

"Got a minute?"

"I'm kind of busy."

"This won't take long."

"OK. Come on in, then, and park your butt in a chair. Can I offer you a drink?"

There was an open bottle of rye sitting on my desk. Flannigan looked longingly at it before answering. "I'm on duty, Frank."

"Some other time, then. What's up?"

"A funny thing happened last night," Flannigan said laconically.

"Oh?" Two could play the game. I knew there was something that Flannigan wanted to tell me, but I wasn't going to make it easy for him.

"Yeah. One of Slim Arneson's hired muscle got himself shot at the Excelsior Hotel."

"Fatally, I hope."

"No such luck. He was just winged," Flannigan said with obvious disappointment. Then, more cheerfully, "Lost quite a bit of blood, though."

"Interesting."

"From what we've been able to piece together the shooter was a guy named Thicke. He and a party named Narcissian were sharing a suite when Arneson's goons broke through the door."

"What did this Thicke have to say?"

"Not much. He and Narcissian appear to have gotten away by way of the fire escape."

"Can't say that I blame them. So are you pitching this as a story idea?"

"Narcissian and Thicke got away, but Arneson's men didn't," Flannigan continued, ignoring the jibe. "The house dick called the cops and an ambulance."

"All very interesting, Pat, but why are you telling me all this? After all, I can read about it in the papers tomorrow morning."

"It's a curious thing, Frank. When we questioned Sven, that's the one that didn't get shot, he insisted that he didn't have a clue who Narcissian or Thicke were and that he didn't have a beef with either one. He and Olaf, that's the one that took the bullet, were looking for a guy goes by the name Charlie Luck. Seems he's a small time gambler."

"You don't say. Sounds like a case of mistaken identity to me."

Flannigan went on ignoring me. "Now the interesting thing is that Sven said that someone had told them that this Charlie Luck was holed up in the Excelsior under the name Narcissian."

"I see. Sounds like they need a better source of information."

"Yeah. But you see, Frank, when I asked who it was that told them, they said it was you."

"Me? Why would I do a thing like that? Besides, I don't hang around with the criminal element anymore. I've gone legit. I'm a writer now. See, it says so on the door."

"That's what I thought, too, Frank, but this Sven stuck to his story. I thought I'd come by and see what you have to say about the whole thing."

Now I could have cooked up some story and lied to Flannigan, but he knew me too well for that to work. So I told him the truth, or enough of it to get him to go away.

"It's like this, Pat. This Narcissian and Thicke came to me the other day with some cockamamie story about how they were looking for a magic coin. A real tall tale out of the

Arabian nights or something. They seemed to think this guy Charlie Luck had gotten a hold of it, and wanted me to get it for them. Now I know Charlie slightly, but I haven't seen him in awhile. I brushed them off just to get them out of my hair. A few days earlier, the Nordic twins had been looking for Charlie, too. I know the Swedes work collection for Arneson, but the word on the street is that it's Arneson that's in to Charlie for a bundle. I figure maybe Arneson is thinking it would be cheaper to kill Charlie than to pay up."

It was Flannigan's turn to be interested. "You know that for a fact, Frank?"

"I'm pretty sure. Anyway, Sven and Olaf stopped me on the street yesterday afternoon asking about Charlie again. It was looking like it might get ugly, so I gave them a line about Charlie being registered at the Excelsior under the name Narcissian. I just wanted them to go away without beating me into the pavement."

"So you sent them to the Excelsior expecting a blow up."

"Would I do that, Pat? I knew they were both looking for the same guy. I thought maybe they could compare notes or something."

"Uh-huh." Flannigan wasn't buying it, but he didn't know enough to poke holes in my story.

"So, did you arrest the Swedes?"

"Nah. It turns out that getting shot ain't a crime in this state. They paid the hotel for the broken door, so they don't want to press charges. We had to let Sven go and Olaf is out of the hospital, though his arm is in a sling."

"Too bad. What about Narcissian and Thicke?"

"There still out there someplace. We're looking for them."

"A pair like that shouldn't be hard to spot."

"We'll get 'em sooner or later," Flannigan drawled. "You know, Frank—"

"Yeah?"

"I don't think this Sven and Olaf are going to be too happy with you for steering them wrong. I'd watch myself if I were you."

"I'll do that, Pat."

"I've got to get going. If you see this Charlie guy, let me know. It sounds like he could use some protection."

Flannigan let himself out. I sat there for a moment, then poured two fingers of rye into the glass. I slammed down the liquor and then unlocked the lower drawer of my desk, the one where I keep my gun. Things were getting serious.

Now, even when I was a P.I. I didn't like to carry a gun on me on the theory that when guns are around people have a habit of getting shot, including me. But there are times when packing a rod just makes sense. The one in the drawer was a .32 automatic. Not much stopping power, but it will slow someone down if you hit them in the right place. It's small and easy to conceal. I checked the action to make sure everything was working and then slipped in a clip. I've got a little holster, too, that you can hardly see when it's clipped to my belt in the small of my back.

I went back to working on *Death Buys a Condo.* Suddenly, how the ending worked out seem to take on greater importance.

I should have known something was wrong when I opened the apartment door. I couldn't smell dinner cooking. If it were true that Ezekial Handler had created Janet, then he had created her as the perfect woman, beautiful, smart, and a wonderful cook. The only time she didn't have dinner in progress when I came home was when we had made plans to go out. Yet, when I opened the door, there were no luscious aromas wafting from the kitchen.

As I entered the living room, I saw her sitting in a chair. There was a tense look on her face. Janet never gets tense, even when a soufflé falls, which for her it never does.

"Frank, we have company," she announced.

Looking around the room I saw Narcissian and Thicke who had been standing where I couldn't see them from the entry hall. Thicke was holding an ugly looking automatic which was pointed at Janet. Narcissian had a delicate little revolver which he was waving around to no particular purpose.

"Ah, Mr. Slade. We meet again," Narcissian said, the revolver suddenly pointed in my direction. "A curious thing happened, Mr. Slade. Two Norse gods barged into our room at the Excelsior. Mr. Thicke was forced to shoot one of them so that we might affect our escape. It seems they were under the misapprehension that Charlie Luck was staying in our room. You wouldn't know anything about that, would you Mr. Slade?"

"Beats me. But then you can't be too careful in a hotel like that."

"Be that as it may, Mr. Slade, I am still looking for this Charlie Luck. In fact, I'm growing desperate to find him. The incident at the Excelsior has made our position in your fair city somewhat precarious. I find myself forced to take actions that may seem a bit precipitous."

"Like invading my home and holding my wife at gun point?"

"Come now, Mr. Slade. We are both men of the world. We know that there are times when we must take certain distasteful actions in order to gain a bit of leverage."

"I'm not sure I would agree with that, Mr. Narcissian."

"Ah, that's what I like about you, Mr. Slade. You are able to hold a divergent opinion while still maintaining a degree of civility. But I digress. Where is Charlie Luck. More importantly, where is the coin?"

"I haven't heard from Charlie in days. That's the truth. He's hiding out because a couple of goons named Sven and Olaf are trying to kill him."

"To get possession of the coin?" Narcissian interjected.

"No. Because their boss owes Charlie a great deal of money, so much money that he thinks that it would be cheaper to kill Charlie than to pay him off."

"But you could get in touch with him if you wanted?"

"Who?"

"Charlie! Charlie Luck, Mr. Slade. Who did you think?"

"I wasn't sure. I thought maybe Slim Arneson. You weren't being very specific."

"Why would I wish to speak with this Slim Arneson?" Narcissian asked with exasperation.

"I thought maybe you might want to apologize."

"I don't understand, Mr. Slade. Apologize for what?"

"For shooting one of his goons. The one named Olaf."

"This is completely besides the point, Mr. Slade. I might well suspect you of trying to buy time, as they put it. What I want is to find this Charlie Luck. I believe that you are the man to arrange matters, and I'm willing to hold your lovely wife hostage until you do so. Do I make myself clear?"

"Well, when you put it that way, yes. But I still don't know where Charlie is or how to get in touch with him."

"That's unfortunate. That means we may have a long wait. I trust that eventually Charlie Luck will contact you."

"Maybe. Maybe not."

"In that case, I suggest you take a seat, Mr. Slade. Oh, I will deprive you of that pistol you are carrying behind your back. We wouldn't want anything unfortunate to happen. I'm afraid that my associate, Mr. Thicke, is prone to shooting when startled."

I handed Narcissian my pistol which he set on the coffee table. I took a seat on the sofa.

"As it appears we may be here for awhile, would either of you gentlemen like refreshments?" Janet asked in the same genteel voice she would have used with a visiting clergyman. "Coffee, perhaps?"

"Tea would be preferable, my dear," Narcissian answered.

"That can be arranged. China or Earl Grey?"

"Earl Grey. And some biscuits would be appreciated. It's been some time since Mr. Thicke and myself have eaten."

Janet stood to go into the kitchen. Thicke looked at Narcissian questioningly.

"Oh, I think we can trust Mrs. Slade not to do anything foolish, Nigel. After all, we do have him 'covered', I believe is the expression."

Janet went into the kitchen from which various noises of water running and drawers clattering could be heard. After a few minutes there was came the whistle of a tea kettle, followed by more kitchen noises.

Eventually, Janet reemerged from the kitchen. She wasn't, however, carrying a tea tray. Instead, she held a Colt .45 automatic and wore a look of grim determination. I'd seen that look before.

"I think it's time you gentlemen leave," she said in a voice that lowered the room temperature several degrees.

"Do you really think you can shoot both of us, Mrs. Slade, before one of us puts a bullet in your husband?" Narcissian queried.

"Yes," Janet said in a frozen monosyllable.

"I would believe her, gentlemen," I said, relaxing against the back of the sofa. "I've seen her do it. She never misses. She's made that way."

Narcissian looked uncertainly into the barrel of the automatic. Nonchalantly I leaned forward and picked up the .32 from where it lay the coffee table. I pointed it at the space between his two piggish eyes.

"Very well, Mr. Slade. You seem to have gotten the better of us for the moment. Nigel. It would seem we are not wanted."

Narcissian stood ponderously and the two of them headed towards the door, their movements followed by two automatic pistols.

After they had left, Janet said, "I'm afraid dinner will be a little late, Frank. Perhaps you might like a drink. I think I could do with one myself."

I was pouring Scotch over ice when the phone rang. Janet answered it, the pistol still held in her other hand.

"It's for you, Frank. The Professor."

I added soda to the drinks and then exchanged one of them for the telephone receiver.

"Is this a bad time, Frank? Your wife sounded a little tense."

"No, it's okay. We just got rid of some unwanted guests." I explained Narcissian's visit and the incident at the Excelsior.

"Has Charlie been in touch with you, Professor?"

"No, I haven't seen or heard from him since we met in your office."

"That's too bad. I'd like to get in touch with him."

"I did hear from my friend at the university."

"Oh. Does this relate to our problem?"

"Possibly. It seems that the topic has interested him and he's been doing some further research. He came across a legend of at least one instance when a holder of the coin was able to divest himself of it without suffering dire consequences."

"Go on. I'm all ears."

"As you know, trying to get rid of the coin by giving it away or simply by losing it typically results in the death of the possessor of the coin. It would appear that Lady Luck doesn't like to be jilted. But there appears to be a loophole. If the coin itself is put up as part of the wager, then it is Lady Luck's decision as to who wins. She makes her choice and doesn't appear to hold a grudge. At least that's what the legend says."

"So if Charlie bets the coin and loses, he's off the hook."

"If you can believe the legend."

"What if Lady Luck has taken a shine to Charlie and he wins?"

"Then he's no worse off. But again, there is a catch."

"Of course. Isn't there always."

"The stakes have to be high and they have to be even. You can't bet the coin against, say, a penny. Lady Luck would feel insulted by the stakes and probably take it out on the coin holder."

"That seems reasonable," I agreed.

"Of course, this is all just legend, Frank. None of it may be true."

"Just like the idea of a lucky coin."

"Exactly."

"Well, thanks, Professor. And if you see Charlie, have him get in touch with me."

"Do I sense a plan forming, Frank?"

"Maybe, just maybe." I hung up and started working out the details.

I did have at least the outline of a plan to get Charlie, and hopefully everyone else, out of the mess he'd gotten himself into, but maddeningly, Charlie, the one indispensable element, had gone missing. He hadn't contact me, hadn't been in touch with the Professor, nor had he been seen in any of his usual haunts.

It was a relief, then, when I heard his voice on the other end of the telephone.

"Charlie, where have you been?" I almost screamed into the instrument. "I've been trying to get in touch."

"It didn't seem like you had much of a plan to help me, Frank, so I decided to skip town for a while," Charlie said. There was a lot of noise in the background, including a garbled announcement that sounded as if it was coming from a loudspeaker. "I took the bus out to Atlantic City. I figured that no one would be looking for me there."

"You've been in Atlantic City? I thought I told you to lay off the gambling."

"I've just been playing the slots. Small time stuff, mostly quarters. But it's no fun if you know you're always going to win. I took in a couple of shows though. That was alright."

Great, I thought. Here I'd been dodging armed thugs and nut cases and Charlie had been watching Sinatra impersonators.

"Where are you now?"

"I'm at the bus depot. I just got back into town. I was hoping that you've figured something out. I can't live like this anymore, Frank."

"I think I've come up with a way out of the whole mess. It will allow you to get rid of the coin without getting dead, and square things with Arneson as well. The thing is though, it's a big gamble and it might not work."

"So what are the odds?"

"As close as I can figure, 50/50."

"Sounds fair to me. You're sure it's not stacked in favor of the house?"

"Not as far as I can see, but then I'm just guessing, Charlie."

"It doesn't seem like I've got much choice, Frank. If I don't do something either Arneson is going to get me or I'll go crazy. What do I have to do?"

I outlined my plan to Charlie and told him to call back in a few hours to give me time to make the arrangements.

My next problem was getting in touch with Arneson. This proved harder than I thought. It's not like he was listed in the Yellow Pages under "Bookies" or "Hoodlums." I made a lot of phone calls to people I knew that played the ponies. One of them finally gave me the number of a bookie that worked for Arneson. I called him and asked him to pass the word on that I wanted to speak to the man himself.

It didn't take long after that. Maybe a half hour had elapsed when the phone in my office rang. It was Arneson.

"So you finally decided to wise up, Slade, and turn over that weasel Charlie Luck?"

"You've got it wrong, Arneson. I'm still acting on Charlie's behalf."

"So why the call, then, Slade? After that trick you played on Sven and Olaf they'd just as soon take you out as Charlie."

"I called because I have a proposition for you."

"A proposition? It don't seem like either you or Charlie are in a position to be making deals."

"I'd think that you'd be more than happy to find a way out of this mess. You're the one who owes Charlie money. Money that we both know you can't pay. A bookie that doesn't pay up on his bets isn't going to be in the business long, is he?"

"OK, Slade. You've made your point. What's this proposition of yours?"

"Charlie wants to make a wager with you. Double or nothing. You win, and you don't owe Charlie a thing. Your business reputation is safe and there'll be no reason for you to kill Charlie."

"And if I lose? What then, Slade?"

"Why, then you'll owe Charlie twice as much as before of course."

"I don't get it, Slade. We both know that I can't pay what I owe him now. Why should he be willing to risk a bet when there's no way that I can pay off if I lose."

"It's a gamble, Arneson. Charlie's a gambler. There's a fifty-fifty chance that things will work out and everyone will be happy If things don't work out—well then Charlie goes into hiding and you're finished in this town for good."

"It still sounds screwy to me, Slade."

"Maybe so, but do you have a choice? Even if you manage to rub Charlie out, the word will get around that you welshed on a bet. And if Charlie does end up dead in some gutter, the cops are going to know who to look for. I'm offering you a way out, Arneson. Are you going to take it?"

"Say I agree to this scheme of yours, how's this bet going to work?"

"Let's keep it simple. I'll get a fresh deck of cards. Still in the box with the seal intact. You each draw a card. High card wins."

"Just like that? One card for a hundred and fifty G's?"

"Just like that."

"And where would this card game take place?"

"My office. Seven o'clock tonight. Just you, me, and Charlie."

"You must be crazy, Slade. So am I, I guess. It's a deal. Seven tonight. I'll be there."

He hung up. I waited for Charlie to call back and set things up when he did. After that, I called Janet to tell her that I'd be home late and not to worry about dinner because I'd get something at the diner on the corner. She wasn't happy about that. She thinks that the food is too greasy. She's probably right. I had a burger and some fries washed down with a beer. On the way back to the office I stopped at the drugstore and picked up a deck of cards. Then I waited until seven rolled around.

Charlie got to my office about fifteen minutes early. The little guy looked nervous as hell. I can't say that I blamed him. The game we were playing was for big stakes, and I'm not talking about the hundred and fifty grand, either.

I motioned him to a chair and offered him a drink, but he refused. Charlie wasn't a drunk, but before the coin had come into his hands, he wouldn't have turned it down.

"How was Atlantic City?" I asked to waste time.

"It's ain't all it's cracked up to be. The casinos got nothing on Vegas. The ocean is okay, though."

I'd never been there, at least that I could remember. I thought that Charlie might have had the right idea. A change of scenery didn't sound half bad. Maybe Janet and I should take a trip when this mess was over which hopefully would be in about half an hour.

Arneson was right on time, but he wasn't alone. Sven and Olaf were with him, Olaf looking a bit the worse for wear with his right arm in a sling.

"I thought I said come alone," I commented.

"Yeah, well I didn't," Arneson responded. "This deal still sounds screwy and I wanted some protection in case you pulled something, Slade. You got a problem with it?"

"It's fine by me, as long as the rules of the game don't change. But just so you don't get any ideas, Lt. Flannigan, a friend of mine, is in a squad car out front along with a couple of uniforms. Anything goes down, and he knows where to look."

"OK. Seems we understand each other. Let's get this over with."

"Suits me." I pulled out a piece of paper and began to write. "How much exactly does Mr. Arneson here owe you, Charlie?"

"A hundred and forty eight thousand three hundred and seventy two dollars."

"Does that sound right, Arneson?"

He looked in a little black book he carried in his jacket pocket. "Yeah, that's the amount."

I wrote it down on the paper. "OK. Here's the wager. Charlie puts up the all the money that you owe him plus one silver dollar. If he wins, you owe him twice that amount. If you win, Arneson, you owe him nothing."

"What's the business of with the silver dollar?" Arneson asked suspiciously.

"That's just to make it interesting. Two bucks ain't going to break you, is it?"

"It's screwy, like the rest of this deal," Arneson complained.

"Are you in?"

"Yeah."

I continued, "The winner is to be determined by whoever draws the highest card. If the drawn cards have the same value a heart beats a spade beats a diamond beats a club. There will be no redraw. Is that agreed?"

"How do I know you haven't stacked the deck?"

"It's a fresh deck. I bought it at the drugstore down the block a couple of hours ago. It's still sealed. You can check it yourself."

I reached into the top drawer of my desk and pulled out the deck, slamming it on the top. Arneson picked it up, looking it over as if it was going to bite him. Seemingly satisfied, he laid it back down on the desk.

"Do you want to check it, Charlie?"

"I trust you Frank."

"Fine. Are you both in agreement about the amount and the rules?" They both nodded. "OK. Sign here." I shoved the piece of paper on which I'd been writing everything down over to Arneson.

Somewhat surprisingly, he pulled out a pair of reading glasses and looked it over. Finally, he signed it and pushed it towards Charlie. Charlie glanced at it and then signed his own name. I noticed that his last name was actually Johnston, not Johnson. He reached into his pocket and pulled out the coin and placed it on top of the paper before passing it back to me.

"Are we ready?"

"Get on with it, Slade."

Nervously I slit the seal on the deck of cards with my finger nail. I fanned them out face up so that everyone could see they were all there. I removed the Jokers and shuffled the deck three times trying hard not to spray the stiff cardboard all over the room.

"Are you satisfied?" There were nods of assent. "OK. You each get to cut the deck once. Charlie, you go first."

Charlie picked a spot at about the middle of the deck, lifted the top of the pack and then put the remaining cards on top. Arneson's cut was a little lower on the deck. I neatened the pile and pushed it to a spot about midway between the two of them.

"Who goes first?" Arneson asked. I could detect a hint of tension behind the tough guy attitude.

"Charlie picks first."

"Why?" Arneson asked, suspicious again.

"Why not? Look, he's the one giving you a way out. I think he deserves the first pick."

Arneson said nothing. Charlie looked at me and I nodded. Gingerly, Charlie picked the top card off the deck and looked at it without showing us. His face went white. Finally, he laid the card down on the table face up. It was the Queen of Hearts. Arneson wasn't too happy either. I watched Sven's hand as it reached into his jacket, but it came out empty.

If there was ever a sign that Lady Luck wasn't going to cooperate with us, this was it. The Queen of Hearts. If there was any card that would serve as a token of Lady Fortuna, this was it. I started to wonder if any of us were going to get out of that room alive.

Arneson licked his lips. He knew the odds were against him. Only eight cards out of the fifty-one that remained on the deck would make him the winner. If he didn't pick one of them he was finished in this town, probably finished anywhere.

Slowly he reached out to the deck and took the top card. Sliding it face down on the desktop he slid it towards him. When it reached the edge of the desk he picked it up to look at it.

Suddenly a crooked smile appeared on his face. He slammed the card down on the desk so we could all see.

"The King of Spades," Arneson announced triumphantly.

The two cards sat face up next to each other. There was no doubt. Arneson had won.

"Congratulations, Mr. Arneson. You're the winner. You owe Charlie exactly nothing." I reached into the desk drawer and pulled out a document to this affect that I had prepared. "Charlie, will you sign this?"

Charlie took the paper and put his signature on it and handed it back to me. Arneson couldn't figure out why Charlie was smiling. I handed him the paper. He looked at it, folded it once and shoved it into his jacket pocket.

"I still say this whole thing is screwy, but I'm not complaining. As far as I'm concerned, we're done. Just don't place any more bets with me, Charlie."

"Don't worry. I won't."

Arneson stood up and made to leave. Sven and Olaf seemed confused by what had just happened, not sure what they were supposed to do next.

"Aren't you forgetting something, Arneson?" I said.

"What's that?" Arneson asked, turning back, expecting a double cross.

"The silver dollar. You won it fair and square."

"You keep it, Slade. Payment for services."

"No, that's not the deal. The coin is yours."

"Suit yourself," the bookie said as he scooped the coin up and dropped it in his pocket without looking at it.

"I'll take that." This was from Narcissian. He and Thicke had just walked in the door with guns drawn. For a moment I thought Olaf was going to jump Thicke, one handed-or not, but Sven reached out a hand to stop him.

"Who are these jokers?" Arneson asked.

"The skinny guy is the one that shot Olaf," Sven supplied. "The old guy was there, too."

"Your henchman is correct, Mr. Arneson. My associate is the one who shot the other Nordic gentleman. You can take that as a warning. We are desperate men and we won't hesitate from taking desperate measures. Now hand over the coin."

"What coin?" Arneson asked. He still was in the dark about Lady Luck's talisman.

"The one that you've just received from Mr. Luck. Hand it over."

Arneson reached into his pocket and came up with the coin. He looked it over, a puzzled expression on his face. "This thing?"

“Yes. That "thing", as you put it. Hand it over.”

That was the point where Flannigan made his appearance along with a couple of patrolmen with guns drawn. There wasn’t much of a struggle and in a moment Thicke and Narcissian were cuffed and on their way downtown.

After their departure, Flannigan took down statements which were singularly uninformative. We all agreed that we didn’t have a clue why the two bandits had broken into the office. After all, there was nothing of value there unless you consider the unfinished manuscript of *Death Buys a Condo* to be worth something.

“Can I go now?” Arneson asked after he had signed his statement.

“Yeah, you can go,” Flannigan said reluctantly. “Just don’t leave town without letting us know. We might need you to testify.”

Arneson left along with Sven and Olaf. Charlie made his apologies and waited just long enough for Arneson to make it out of the building before departing.

“So what just happened here, Frank?” Flannigan asked when we were alone.

“Nothing. Nothing at all.”

“So what was with the two foreigners?”

“You’ve got me, Pat. They seemed to have thought that Charlie had something valuable, some sort of antiquity. But Charlie’s just a little guy who likes to play the ponies on occasion. He certainly didn’t have anything like that.”

“So, are you going to press charges?”

“I think not. But you might have ballistics check the pistol the skinny guy was carrying. You might find the results interesting if you compared them to other recent crimes.”

“Have it your way, then. Say hello to Janet for me.”

After that, Charlie went back to being a small time player of the ponies, losing about as much as he won. He's never been happier. Towards the start of November I got a postcard from him. It was a picture of a race track in San Diego. On the back he'd written "I thought I'd try my luck in California. Best Wishes, Charlie."

Thicke went to prison for shooting Olaf. Narcissian went back to wherever he came from, I guess. At least I never heard of him again. As far as Arneson, well, nobody had warned him about not giving the coin away. He must have passed it to someone thinking it was worthless. A week after the bet with Charlie a garbage truck ran over him backing out of an alley. He died instantly. Lady Luck doesn't like to be dumped.

So that's the end of the story as far as I'm concerned. You can believe it or not. I'm not sure that I do. After all, is there such a being as Lady Luck? Just one word of advice, though. Check your change before you accept it.

Bonus Story

A Wolf in Sheep's Clothing
By Greg Fowlkes

From the Book

Trial by Magic
~ Tales from the Casebook of The Wizard at Law ~

A Wolf in Sheep's Clothing

The dark clouds scudded across the sky, occasionally parting to reveal the bright orb of the full moon. The wolf's ears pricked as he ran through the woods. The deer, a fat buck, was running ahead of him, crashing through the underbrush. The buck was wounded and there was the scent of blood in the crisp night air.

There was another sound, too, and a smell. Man! The wolf wasn't the only hunter that night. The man was after the deer, as well. But the wolf wasn't afraid, and he was hungry, too.

The deer was closer. The wolf quickened his pace, running faster than the man. He would get to the prey first. Suddenly the deer stopped, exhausted, bleeding, and turned to face the wolf in one last stand. A leap, fangs closing on the throat, the deer down, struggling and then lying still.

The wolf had just begun to feed when the man came up. He turned, fangs bared, a snarl rising from his chest.

"Damn wolf," the Man said. He was big for a human, and still strong despite his age. And there was a smell of power about him that the wolf knew was not natural. But there was another smell about him, too, a sweet smell the wolf couldn't place.

"Thas my deer, Mr. Wolfie," the man said, his words slurred by alcohol. The wolf snarled in response.

"Back off, Wolf. You don't know what your messing with." The wolf crouched, readying himself for a lunge at the man. But the man wasn't afraid. He straightened up, somehow seeming even taller, taller than a Man had any right to be. There was fire in his eyes, and the man began to chant. As if on cue, the clouds parted and the wolf found himself caught in a beam of moonlight.

When the wolf awoke he was cold, shivering. That was odd as the night had not been cold. He felt strange, confused. He sniffed the night air, but his nose didn't seem to be working right. He tried to stand, but his muscles didn't respond the way they should. He looked at his paw, but it wasn't a paw. It was a man's hand. Struggling to get his legs under him, the man who had been a wolf sat on his haunches and howled at the full moon.

It was a full moon. Egil disliked full moons. You never knew what might come out, and Egil, more than most, had a good idea of the possibilities. Though currently a lawyer with a small but improving practice, he had done his undergraduate work at the California Institute of Thaumaturgy, the best school of magic in the country. He was only too aware of the various and often dangerous beings that could cross over from the half world on nights when the moon was full. Not to mention the effects the lunar orb had on many of the denizens of this world. The term "lunatic" was firmly grounded in scientific reality.

That was why Egil took note when the hairs on the back of his hand stood at attention. He sniffed the air intently. It's a little known fact among laymen that many supranatural phenomenon produce distinctive odors detectable to a trained nose. Egil was by no means a "witch finder," but he had enough training and experience to detect the most obvious threats, and he didn't like what he was sensing. It was similar, but not identical to, the taint of a werewolf. He sat up straight in his desk chair looking expectantly at the frosted glass panel set in his office door.

A moment later the shadow of a human form appeared silhouetted by the hall light. A hand reached up and knocked on the door frame.

"Hello, is anyone here? I'm looking for Egil Njalsson, the lawyer."

"Come in," Egil said, somewhat reluctantly. If he had been expecting a vampire he would not have offered the invitation, but with a werewolf the old restriction against entering uninvited was powerless.

The door opened and a young man entered tentatively. He was small, barely five feet and didn't look to weigh more than a hundred pounds. He had eyes of an extraordinary piercing pale blue. He might easily have been taken for a boy, but there was a wiry strength about his lean, sinewy body that indicated he might be a dangerous foe if pushed. There was also no doubt that the "were" emanation was arising from him.

"Are you Egil Njalsson, the lawyer?" the young man asked.

"I am. What can I do for you?" Egil asked carefully.

"I'm in need of some legal help, and I've heard that you have experience with cases that are, shall we say, out of the norm."

Egil wondered, not for the first time, if having his reputation was a good thing. It certainly had brought him a number of clients who paid well, but not without risk.

"Have a seat. What exactly can I do for you Mr.—?"

"Thank you," the client said seating himself but not offering his name.

"Excuse me, but you are a werewolf, aren't you?"

"Not exactly."

"What exactly are you? If I am going to take you on as a client, I will need to know what I'm dealing with."

"I'm, for want of a better term, a were-human."

"A were-human?" Egil asked with surprise. He had thought he was up on the lore, but this was a new one for him.

"The fact is, that I am not a human. I am a wolf that turns into a man every full moon."

Egil had never heard of such a thing, but for the moment he decided to suspend his disbelief. His nose, at least, seemed to indicate that there was something unusual about the slight man that sat in the chair opposite him.

"If you don't mind my asking, how exactly did your condition come about?"

The were-man sighed. "It was a curse. A Native American shaman, Ojibawa I think. He was drunk. We had been hunting the same deer during a full moon. I got there first. He cursed me. I turned into a man. And every full moon since I turn into a man for a period three to five days."

"Do you mind my asking, if you are a wolf, how you come to speak English so well?"

"I can't tell you. All I know is that when I am in the form of a man I have all the knowledge you would expect a man to have. I can speak English, I can read, I even speak Ojibawa. When I return to being a wolf, I lose those abilities."

"And the shaman? Have you approached him about undoing the curse?"

"He died. He drowned when his canoe overturned that same night. As I said, he was drunk. I've approached others about my plight, but no one seems to have any knowledge of such a curse or how to undo it. As you can imagine, the transformation is inconvenient and unpleasant. I don't want to be a man. I was quite happy being a wolf. Being a man is so complicated."

"I might know someone who could help. I'll mention it to him. But I take it you came to me about a legal problem and not your curse."

"Yes. If I am going to keep turning into a man, I need someplace to stay. Someplace I can store clothing and other things I need as a man. There's a small plot of woodlands with a cabin that I would like to purchase. I have some money coming to me, but as a wolf, there's no way that I can complete the transaction."

"I see," Egil said. He wasn't sure he wanted to know how a wolf came by enough money to buy a cabin, but as a lawyer he knew enough not to ask questions that he didn't want to hear the answers to.

"I'll have to do some research, but I might be able to arrange a trust of some sort that would be legally empowered to own the property, pay taxes and handle any other financial matters that might arise. I can set things up so that I have power to conduct any necessary transactions."

"That sounds like it would be acceptable,"

Egil thought that for a wolf, his client seemed particularly well organized and businesslike. Egil got the particulars of the property, who the current owner was, and the sale price.

"It will take me a few days to arrange the paperwork. I don't suppose there is any way for me to contact you?"

"Not for the next month. But if you will get the paperwork together, I will call on you in four weeks time."

"That should be ok. I will arrange to be here. Is there anything else?"

"No. I'll be on my way." The were-man rose abruptly and went to the door.

"Just for convenience, what should I call you?"

The were-man paused in the doorway and thought for a moment, then said, "You can call me Wolfe, John Q. Wolfe." He smiled, revealing a set of very prominent set of teeth, and then left.

Now this wasn't the first time something strange had walked into Egil's office. In fact, it seemed to happen with disconcerting regularity. But the concept of a were-human was a new one to him; something beyond his experience and training. Before he proceeded, he felt the need for some expert advice, and experts never came free. He opened the lower drawer of his desk and withdrew an unopened bottle of Irish whisky.

The sign on the run-down shop said antiques, but Egil knew better. Most of the contents of the shop were just junk, and Egil doubted if the proprietor ever sold any of it. Mostly, it just served as window dressing, providing a cover for the real business that went on in the back room.

Finding the front door unlocked, Egil entered. A tiny bell over the door tinkled as it shut behind him, and a voice from the back cried out, "I'll be with you in a minute."

"Don't rush, it's only me," the lawyer responded.

A few minutes later the proprietor of the store came out of the back room escorting a middle-aged woman dressed in a prim black dress, the sort of thing she might wear to a funeral.

Turning to face the old man at her elbow, she said, "Thank you, again, Mr. Smith. I always feel so much better after our sessions. Same time next month?"

"That will be fine, Mrs. Benjamin. I'm always glad to be of help. Just remember what I told you, you must be on guard against charlatans that want to take your money."

"Oh, I will, Mr. Smith. Don't you worry about that." After taking a long, hard look at Njalsson, she left through the front door.

The old man waved, and then turning to the lawyer said, "Oh, don't give me your disapproving look. There's no harm in what I do. For ten dollars once a month, I give her tea and biscuits and tell her what she wants to hear. So I read the cards and maybe gaze into a crystal ball. It's all harmless entertainment, and it keeps her from doing anything foolish. You know there are people out there who would love to separate a widow from her money."

"I'm sure," Egil said with a chuckle. It was true that Old Jack, or Jakob Schmidts, or whatever name the old man was using that month did a small trade in telling fortunes and providing potions and protective charms, but he always operated in what he, at least, considered an ethical manner. And the charms, unlike many, were the real deal.

"So what brings my favorite counselor to this humble abode? What sort of trouble have you gotten yourself into this time?"

"No trouble. It's just that I've taken on an unusual client and I'm looking for some background information."

"Sounds intriguing. Why don't we retire to the inner sanctum. I trust you've brought a little something to lubricate the brain cells."

Egil brought out the fifth of whisky from his coat pocket and handed it to the old man.

"You're a good lad, Egil. Not many respect their elders the way they should," he said as he parted the curtain that hung on the doorway to the back room.

If the front room was a jumble; the backroom was, in complete contrast, neat as a pin. Two walls were covered with a rank of bookcases filled with a miscellany of volumes, while another held a collection of old photographs. The books, which Egil knew from previous examinations, ranged in age from a few years to a dozen centuries and constituted one of the best libraries of magical works in the country.

In the middle of the room was a simple table covered with a black cloth and with two chairs facing each other. In the middle of the table was an object about eight inches high covered by a velvet cover. Egil knew that underneath the cover was a crystal ball. A deck of Tarot cards sat neatly to the side. There was also a tea pot, two cups, and a small plate of cookies.

"Give me just a minute to clean up," Jack said, setting down the whisky bottle and picking up the tea pot. "Make yourself at home." He retreated up a narrow staircase at the back of the room to the kitchen above. A moment later he returned with two crystal tumblers. With a flourish he opened the bottle and poured three fingers of the amber liquid into each glass.

He pushed one of the glasses over to Egil. "Slange," he said sipping from his own tumbler.

Egil's friend had taken on the persona of an Irish gypsy horse-trader this month, the last of a long line of travelers occupied in that trade. Of course, the previous month he had claimed to be an Indian swami, and the month before that a Tibetan monk. The month before, he couldn't remember. Whatever the story, he maintained the fiction flawlessly, changing his accent and mannerisms to match. Egil wondered what his customers thought of the changes, but he suspected they thought he was just channeling different spirits.

Of course, looking at the wall of photos, he remembered seeing one of a gypsy caravan from the late 1800's. The man holding the reins of the horses bore more than a passing resemblance to the man sitting across the table from him. The picture next to that was a group photo of some rabbis in Vienna back before the breakup of the Austro-Hungarian Empire. The third rabbi from the left, if one allowed for the beard and side curls, looked a lot like Jack. There was also one of a group of Indians and Army officers taken at the signing of a peace treaty. Jack's face stared out from underneath the buffalo headdress of an Comanche shaman standing in the back row. Egil never had been able to get a straight or consistent answer about Jack's origins. He was certain that the man was older than he looked, which was saying something, but just how much older was an open question.

"So, tell me about this client."

"Have you ever heard of a were-human? I don't mean a were-wolf or anything like that, I mean an animal that gets turned into a man every full moon."

"That's a good one, Egil. You really know how to think them up."

"I'm serious. Is it possible?"

"Tell me what this man looked like?" Jack said, suddenly at attention.

"He was thin, maybe a hundred pounds or so. Lean and muscular. The backs of his hands were quite hairy as was his neck. His ears had a hint of a point to them. He had pale blue eyes."

"That certainly sounds like the real thing. The hair and the pointy ears you might expect from the wolf nature. The weight makes sense, too. After all, a full grown wolf doesn't weigh nearly as much as a man. Mass would have to be conserved in any transformation. Let me think a bit."

Jack took a distracted sip of whisky. "I seem to remember reading something once. Now where was it." He got up and started to look over the volumes in his bookshelf. "Ah, yes, I think this is it," as he pulled out a slim leather bound volume that looked as if it could be three or four hundred years old. "Lucian of Parma," he said. "It's in Latin, but the title translates to something like 'Strange Occurances.' There's a case he reports of in Dalmatia, about 450 A. D. or so. Of course Lucian was writing several centuries later, but he was using some old church records."

He thumbed through the book until he came to the passage he was interested in. "I won't translate the whole thing. Basically, it's a report of a naked man being found by a bunch of villagers. He acted crazy and he didn't seem to understand any language. They locked him up in a room of the church while they decided what to do with him. The priest who wrote the original account said that this happened during the full of the moon and that he thought the man might be a lunatic. Anyway, they kept him locked up for a few days. But on the third day, when they went to take him some food and water, they found the man gone and a wolf in his place. The wolf got loose and ran away. But for several months after that, during the full moon, the villagers reported seeing a naked man running on all fours and howling pitifully. Meanwhile, a wolf had been plaguing the villagers, attacking sheep and such. They finally cornered the wolf and killed it. After that there were no more appearances of the naked man."

"So you think the man was actually the wolf?"

"Could be. Lucian is kind of vague on that. He's just recounting the story. But he does say that at about the same time, there was a powerful sorcerer operating in the neighborhood. He speculates that perhaps this sorcerer cast a spell on the wolf just to cause trouble. How does your man-wolf explain his condition? I take it he does talk?"

"Actually, he spoke quite well, and seemed quite rational. He claimed that a drunken Native American shaman put a curse on him one night when they were hunting the same deer. The shaman drowned the same night when he fell out of his canoe, thus he can't undo the curse. This happened up in the northern part of the state."

"I see. I've heard of a powerful shaman operating up there, though I've never crossed paths with him. From rumors, he might have been strong enough to pull something like this off."

"I don't suppose there is any way to remove the curse? My client would rather remain a wolf full time."

"Very sensible of him," Jack commented. "I'm afraid this is kind of beyond me. A curse like that is very dark magic indeed. Without knowing the specifics it would be nearly impossible to counter act it. I'm afraid your client will just have to live with it."

"He seems resigned to that possibility. He actually seemed very intelligent and civilized. For a wolf."

"Just what did he want you to do for him? If you don't mind my asking."

"If he's going to keep turning into a man, he wants to buy a cabin where he can hole up during the full moon. A place where he can keep his clothes during the part of the month when he's not a man."

"Sounds sensible. Do you think you can do it?"

"He says he has enough money to buy the place. I'm not sure how a wolf could come up with that kind of cash. The problem is, how do I put it in his name? I'm thinking of setting up some kind of trust with me as the administrator. That way I could take care of the taxes and things without his name being involved."

"Well, you're the lawyer. I'm sorry about the other. I'll keep looking, but I wouldn't hold out much hope. Another drink?"

"No, I have to get going. I've got a court date tomorrow."

☆ ☆ ☆ ☆ ☆

Over the next few weeks, Egil followed up on the property his client wanted. It was certainly on the market, and when he contacted the real estate agent he seemed more than eager to accept an offer at the price the wolf had mentioned. He had started to draw up the papers for a trust, but the question of ownership still posed a problem. The trust had to have some owner of record. He was reading up on the matter one night when there came a knock at his office door.

"Come in," he said.

The door opened to reveal two men, obviously Native Americans. They both appeared to be in their late forties or early fifties, about six feet and each over two hundred pounds. They were dressed in suits, though they looked more like off the rack at Sears than Saville Row, and wore string ties with silver clips. Neither one looked particularly comfortable in the outfits, as if they were more accustomed to life outdoors than in offices.

"Are you Mr. Njalsson, the lawyer?" the elder of the two asked.

"Yes, that's me. What can I do for you gentlemen?"

"My name is John White Eagle and this is Charlie Loon. We represent the Wolf Lake Band from up north. It's our understanding that you are interested in a certain property in our neck of the woods, and we have a few questions for you, if you don't mind."

"I'll have to hear the questions first. You have to understand that I have to respect the interests of my client."

"But you are interested in buying the old Jensen place? The realtor said as much."

"That much obviously isn't a secret. I have been empowered by my client to purchase the property."

"Could you tell us what your client means to do with it?"

"May I ask why you are so interested? Is there some conflict of title or claim on the property?"

This question seemed to cause a bit of consternation in the two. "Oh, no. It's nothing like that. It's just that, like I said, we represent the Wolf Lake Band. It's not one of your better known tribes. We only have about four hundred members. We've got a little casino. Doesn't make us much money, but it does provide jobs for thirty or forty of our people and a few of the locals. The rest of the tribe mostly survives hunting and fishing like our ancestors. Well, we're just concerned with anything that might interfere with either of those. You can understand that."

By this time White Eagle was sounding downright apologetic. Egil relaxed a little. He was beginning to think that these two, rather than being hired muscle meant to intimidate him, were just two big guys.

"Without revealing too much about my client, I think I can put your minds at rest. My understanding is that my client is only interested in using the property as a kind of retreat where he can spend a few days of each month in seclusion. I am sure he does not want to open a rival casino or do anything else that might be detrimental to the interests of your tribe."

"That does let us breathe easier, Mr. Njalsson. We're a pretty easy going bunch up north, but lately, well there's been some bad stuff going on. Drugs you know, people coming in and growing marijuana or making that meth stuff. They got guns, and not for hunting. Charlie and I, well we're just concerned with keeping everyone safe."

"I can assure you my client is in no way associated with the trade in illegal drugs."

"That's good, then," White Eagle said.

"Is there anything else I can do for you?" Egil asked.

"No. We appreciate your time, Mr. Njalsson," White Eagle replied and started for the door. But before he could reach for the handle, Charlie Loon gave him a nudge.

"Well, there is one more thing. I know you may think this is crazy, but is your client by any chance a wolf?" White Eagle asked this with a sheepish grin and a shrug of his shoulders.

"What exactly do you mean by that?" Egil asked.

"Well, there have been certain rumors. Not everyone believes them, of course, but our people are maybe a little more open to things like that."

"And if my client were a wolf?"

White Eagle looked down at his feet nervously. "Well, if he is, well, then, I would like to say on behalf of the Wolf Lake Band that we are really, really sorry about what happened."

Egil looked at the pair. "I think you gentlemen should take a seat and explain exactly what you are talking about."

"Then your client is a wolf that has been turned into a man?"

"Let's, for the sake of argument you understand, say that that is the case."

"Well, then it's possible, for the sake of argument, that a former member of the Wolf Lake Band may just possible have been responsible. Mind you, this was without the consent and against the desires of the other members of the tribe."

"I find myself very interested in this hypothetical legend. Please go on."

"Well, Charlie here can probably tell it better than I can."

Charlie Loon sat up straight in his chair before he began his tale. "Among the white man there are tales of such a thing as the seventh son of a seventh son. Such a man might have unusual powers. Well, our people also have such a thing. There was a man, a shaman in our tribe. His father had been shaman as had his father and his father before him since long before our people came to these lands from out east. This family of shamans were powerful men, with each shaman passing on his knowledge to his son for generations. You'd call them wizards. These wizards have been part of our tribe, but separate from ordinary men. They pretty much did whatever they wanted, but because they protected the tribe they were tolerated even when they did some bad things.

"Well, the last of these shamans was a man called Harold Bad Moon, and he was the most powerful of all. I won't say he was a bad man, but he would take what he wanted without asking, he drank too much, and he liked to play practical jokes." He said this last as if it was the worst crime ever.

"Well, there was this buck that he had been hunting. He really wanted that buck, but because he drank too much he wasn't having much luck. When he finally caught up with the buck he found this big wolf had got there before him and killed it and was feeding off it. Well Bad Moon, he got mad, and he cursed the wolf. He said that if he wanted a man's deer, then he could be a man. And after that, every full moon the wolf was turned into a man. That same night, though, Harold Bad Moon was crossing the lake in his canoe and it tipped over and he was too drunk to save himself and he drowned."

"Now you have to understand, Mr. Njalsson," White Eagle interrupted. "My people have nothing against wolves and this wolf in particular. They are part of nature, just like the deer and the muskie. And we feel real bad about any inconvenience that may have been caused him. But there is nothing that we can do to change things back. Honest Injun."

"I have to tell you, that the story you've told me pretty much conforms to what my client says. I also want to say that he doesn't appear to bear any ill-will towards your people in general. His main interest is just surviving the periods when he is a man."

"If there is anything we can do, Mr. Njalsson, let us know. We'd be happy to make things right."

"In fact, there is something you can do. I've been working on setting up a trust to maintain the property in question, but there is an issue of who would hold the title. Now if I structured things so that the trust held the property for the Wolf Lake Band, that would solve that problem. I would be named the administrator of the trust to look after my client's interests. I would also structure things so that ownership of the land would revert to the tribe upon the death of my client. Would you find that acceptable?"

Charlie Loon and John White Eagle looked at each other and nodded. "That would be just fine with us, Mr. Njalsson."

"Good. Then I will draw up the papers and consult with my client. I should be able to finalize everything right after the next full moon."

☆ ☆ ☆ ☆ ☆

By the next full moon, Egil had completed the paperwork for the trust and the papers ready for the client to sign. He had them sitting on his desk in front of him when almost as if on cue the were-man knocked on his door.

"Do you have things arranged?" his client asked.

"Yes, all I need is your signature and the funds to pay for the purchase."

The wolf reached inside the light jacket he was wearing and pulling out an envelope handed it to the lawyer.

Egil opened it and examined the contents. It was a certified check for $20,000 drawn on the Justice Department and made out to Egil Njalsson acting for John Q. Wolfe.

"Is it ok?"

"Yes, it seems to be in order. Do you care to tell me how the government came to owe you this much money?"

"It's reward money. I told them about some drug dealers that were using national forest land to grow marijuana and make drugs."

Egil raised his eyebrow. "You don't mess around, do you?"

"They were scaring all the game. Made it hard to hunt. When can I have the cabin?"

"I'll cash this check in the morning. I've already contacted the owner and he's ready to close as soon as the money is available. He seems in a hurry to sell."

"Things have been getting dangerous up there."

"All I need is your signature on these papers. You can write your name, can't you?"

"Yes. And read, too, as I told you earlier. I don't know how. I just can, while I'm a man."

"Good. I've organized things as a trust. Technically, the property will be owned by the Wolf Lake band of Indians.

You will have the use and control of the lands for the next fifty years or until you die. After that, the property reverts to the Wolf Lake Band. Having the title in the name of the Indians simplifies things quite a bit and offers some additional protections that you wouldn't have if you owned it out right. Under the law, the parcel will be considered Indian lands. It also makes it exempt from property taxes. You don't have a problem with that arrangement, do you?"

"As long as I can use the cabin when I need to and nobody bothers me, I'm ok. I don't have a beef with the Wolf Lake people They've never been a problem except that once."

"They're really sorry about that, by the way. Bad Moon, the shaman that cursed you, was acting on his own. They never had much control over his actions."

"About that. You said you were going to talk to someone. See if he could undo the curse so I'd be a wolf all the time."

"Yeah. I asked him about your case. He said there wasn't much he could do without knowing what exact spell was used. And since this Bad Moon is dead, that may not be possible. He's going to do some more research, but he's not holding out much hope. And he'd know if anyone would. He's the best man I know of for traditional forms of magic."

"Well, thanks for trying. Is there anything more for me to do? About the cabin, I mean. Otherwise, I've got to get going. It's a long way back north."

"Are you going to walk all the way back?"

"No. That's a long way. I'll try to hitch a ride."

"Good luck then. I'll leave a copy of the papers at the cabin after the deal is complete"

"Good bye."

☆ ☆ ☆ ☆ ☆

It was three in the morning when Egil's phone rang. He picked it up groggily and answered "Who is this?"

The voice on the other end responded in a tired but official sounding manner, "Is this Egil Njalsson the lawyer?" Egil was starting to get real tired of that question.

"Yes it is. Who is this?"

"This is Sheriff Olaf Pederson. Do you know a John Q. Wolfe?"

"Yes, he's a client of mine. What's the matter. Has something happened to him?"

"There's been an incident at a local establishment. Your client was involved. I've got him down at the jail right now."

"Has he been arrested?" Egil said with some alarm.

"No. At least not yet. Maybe not at all. But I'd like to get things sorted out. Is there any way that you could come up here so we could talk in person?"

"I think my calendar is clear this morning," Egil said. Not that he was all that busy. "Just what county are you in?"

The sheriff told him and gave directions. It was about a two hour drive north.

The Sheriff's department was a door at the back of a courthouse that looked like it had been built as a public works project during the Depression. There were two patrol cars in the parking lot that weren't quite as old, but were a few years shy of being late model. The door opened when Egil tried it. Inside was a large room with a couple of desks, a radio, and the other accessories of a small town police force. A middle-aged man in a uniform was sitting at one of the desks working on a report. He looked up when Egil walked in.

"Mr. Njalsson? Thanks for coming. Would you care for some coffee. It's not good, but it's strong."

"Yes, I'd like that. It's a long drive. How is my client?"

"He's ok. He's taking a nap in one of the cells. He's not under arrest. It's just the only place we had to put him while we waited."

"So what happened?" Egil asked.

"As far as I've been able to piece together, your client, Mr. Wolfe, had been hitching a ride to his place up north and got dropped here in town. He went into a local bar to order something to eat. While he was waiting for his food a couple of local toughs started picking on him about his size. The bartender said he tried to ignore them, but they kept at it. They were pretty drunk. Well, finally one of them went too far, I guess. Your client pushed back and the guy took a swing at him. That's when the fight broke out."

"Is he hurt?" Egil asked. He knew were-wolves were pretty strong and nearly invulnerable while in wolf form, but he didn't have a clue how things worked with a were-man.

"Other than a few cuts, no. I can't say the same for the other two, though. One's got a broken jaw and a dislocated shoulder and a couple of broken ribs, and the other is worse off. Your friend nearly bit his throat out. You wouldn't think he'd have it in him. I mean he can't weigh more than a hundred pounds if that, but he fought like a wild animal."

"It sounds like he was only acting in self-defense, though."

"That's pretty much the way I've got it figured, too. And there were enough witnesses to back him up. The problem is, those two toughs got some friends that aren't too happy. I'm worried about what might happen if I turn your client loose in town here. That's why I was hoping you'd maybe be able to drive him where he's going to avoid any more trouble."

"I might as well. I'm up here anyway, and I do have some business up by Wolf Lake."

"Good. I'm glad that's taken care of. I'll go get your boy for you."

A minute later the sheriff was back with the wolf. His jacket was ripped and there was some blood on his jeans, but he didn't seem the worse for wear.

The sheriff sent them off with a "I wouldn't waste any time getting out of town." Egil got his client into the car and then headed up the highway to Wolf Lake.

It was almost nine by the time they pulled into the little town that hugged the south shore of the lake. There was a tiny diner that served big plates of eggs, bacon, and hash-browns. While his client was wolfing down his breakfast, Charlie Loon came into the diner for a cup of coffee. If he was surprised to see them he didn't show it. Egil introduced them and they all shook hands around. According to Charlie, the realtor's office was open. While his client was finishing his breakfast, Egil went over to the realtor, closed the deal, and got the keys to the cabin.

He dropped his client off on his way out of town. The cabin wasn't much, mostly a roof and four walls. No electricity, no phone, no driveway out to the road, but then the wolf didn't have a car. He handed him the keys to the cabin and they said their good-byes. Egil didn't expect that he'd ever see the were-man again.

Several months passed, during which Egil's attention was occupied by other matters. The business of the were-man had had receded and been replaced by other cases. He frankly expected that he would never have to deal with it again except for occasional duties related to the trust he had set up.

He was surprised, therefore, when he received a call from Charlie Loon as he worked in his office one afternoon.

"Mr. Njalsson, I thought I'd better tell you that there are some men up here and they're after your client, Mr. Wolfe. They've got guns and I think they mean to kill him."

"Men with guns? Have you told the police?" Egil asked.

"Well, that's just it. There's only the sheriff and a couple of deputies up here. These guys look to be professionals, and if you ask me, not all of them are human."

"Just what do you mean by 'not human'?"

"I'm no shaman, but I picked up a little from my grandfather. I think these guys might be demons."

"Why would demons be after someone who for all intents and purpose is a wolf?"

"It's them drug dealers that he informed on. I think they found out who did it and are out for revenge. There have been rumors going around that the big boss behind the gang is some kind of demon."

"And just what do you expect me to do about it? I'm a lawyer, not a policeman or a demon slayer."

"I don't know. I just thought you should know. Look, we're all scared up here. Bad Moon might have been a drunk and a bully, but he was one heck of a shaman and he always took care of things like this. Now that he went and got himself drowned, we don't have anybody else to turn to. I don't think these guys are going to care one bit if a few Indians get caught in the crossfire. Like I said, I just thought you should know."

"Thanks. And Mr. Loon, if those are demons up there, keep your head down and stay out of their way. You just aren't equipped to fight them."

"Don't I know," the other said before hanging up. Charlie Loon sounded scared, and he had every right to be. The question was, what could Egil do about it. True, he had confronted demons and other denizens of the half world on more than one occasion, but it was not something he relished. Still, he had some obligation to protect his client. What he needed to do was talk to Jack.

Ordinarily, Jack didn't like to talk over the phone. He said that phones were too susceptible to outside influences. Egil suspected that he just wasn't comfortable with modern technology. However, when he found out the cause, he spoke readily enough.

"Do you think it's as bad as he claims?" Jack asked.

"I don't think that Charlie Loon or John White Eagle are the kind of men who scare easily. If they thought they could handle it on their own, they would."

"That's what I was afraid of. It's three days till the full moon. As long as your friend is in wolf form, he's probably safe. Catching a wolf isn't an easy thing, even for a demon. But once he turns into a man, he's going to be in danger. I think we should go up there. How soon can we get there?"

"I was afraid of that. It'll take me a couple of hours to get my gear together. I suspect we should be prepared for a tramp through the woods. Another four or five hours to drive up there. Can you be ready for me to pick you up in two hours?"

"I'll be ready."

Jack was out on the curb in front of his shop when Egil pulled up. He was dressed in boots, jeans, and a warm jacket like he was ready to go duck hunting. He had his usual bag of goodies where he kept his magical gear. He also had what looked like a gun case. Egil was surprised by that. He had never known his friend to use a fire arm of any sort before. Swords, knives, axes, yes, but not guns.

As Jack got in next to him after stowing his gear in the back seat, Egil noticed that he had made one of his changes in persona. It wasn't anything obvious, but despite the fact that he was still recognizably Jack, he now gave the impression that he was a Native American rather than the Irish gypsy he had been the last few months. The cadence of his speech had changed, too, to reflect the new identity. Egil knew that if he looked, he would find that Jack would be wearing a medicine pouch somewhere on his body. When Jack made one of these transformations he was incredibly thorough about it. He wasn't just wearing a disguise, he had become the new person, in this case, a Native American shaman.

They drove in silence as they headed north. While Jack would talk at length when sitting around his rooms sharing a drink he was never loquacious when on business, but now, as a shaman he seemed even more taciturn than usual. Egil took that as a bad sign. Things were going to get dangerous.

It was nearly midnight when they pulled into the little village of Wolf Lake. It was a clear, crisp night and the full moon was high over head. The only lights on in the village were those of the diner. As Egil wasn't sure he could find his client's cabin in the dark and he wasn't sure what they'd find out in the woods, it seemed a good idea to stop there and see if someone could tell them what was going on.

Fortunately, John White Eagle and Charlie Loon were in the diner talking to a group of men, both white and Native American. One thing they all had in common was the worried looks on their faces. One of the men wore a uniform and a badge and looked even more worried than the others.

John White Eagle looked up to see who the newcomers were. When he saw that it was Egil he came over and greeted them.

"Thanks for coming, Mr. Njalsson. I'm glad you're here. We're worried sick. We heard a bunch of gunfire out in the woods, but to tell the truth, we're all too scared to go out there."

"Any word from my client?" Egil asked. As he wasn't sure how many of the other men in the room were aware of his client's true nature, he thought the neutral reference best.

"Not since these out-of-towners showed up."

"Whose your friend?" Charlie Loon asked, suspiciously. He had joined them by the door. Once they had realized that White Eagle knew them, the rest of the men in the diner had ignored them.

"This is Jack. He's a shaman, a good one. He's here to help."

"I don't recognize the tribe," Charlie said. "You're not from around here, are you?"

"You've heard of the 'Last of the Mohicans?'" Jack responded. "I'm the next to the last, and, no, I'm not from around here."

Something about his manner both assuaged Charlie Loon's suspicions and suggested that he should mind his manners around this new shaman.

"No offense. We're just all on edge."

"None taken," Jack said with a chilling grin.

"I'd like to check up on my client, but I'm not sure I can find his place in the dark. I don't think I should wait until morning," Egil said.

"I can get you out there if you've got a car," White Eagle said. He at least seemed to take heart with the presence of Jack.

"It's right out front."

"Let's go, then. I'll just get my gun." He picked up a shotgun that had been laying on the diner's counter.

They exited the diner. White Eagle got in the front passenger seat while Jack climbed in the rear. Charlie Loon got in on the other side. "I told the others to hang tight till we got back to them."

Once they left the dim light of the village's two street lights the night got incredibly dark. Egil was a city boy, and was used to there always being some light. All he could see was a narrow cone provided by the headlights. The trees on either side of the narrow road seemed to be closing in on them. He was driving at twenty-five and still seemed like he was speeding. At any moment he expected something to pop out of the darkness at them.

At that rate, it took them fifteen minutes to reach the wolf's cabin. Charlie Loon had a big flashlight and led the way on the overgrown path to the cabin.

Egil knocked on the door of the cabin. "Mr. Wolfe? It's Egil Njalsson, your lawyer. Are you in there?"

They could hear a rustling inside the cabin. The door edged open an inch and a luminous eye peered out at them. "Who are the others?"

Egil made quick introductions, "This is Jack, an associate of mine. The other two are John White Eagle and Charlie Loon from the Wolf Lake band. We're here to help."

The manwolf opened the door to let them in. The cabin was dark, but he fumbled with some matches and lit a kerosene lamp. Egil noticed there was a blotch of what looked like blood on the side of his client's shirt.

"Are you ok?"

"I seem to be, now. They shot me. I felt the pain and smelled blood, but when I got back to the cabin it seemed to have healed."

"That's to be expected," Jack said. "When in the were state you possess incredible healing powers, making you practically immortal. However, if the bullet had been silver you would probably be dead now. Of course, once the full moon is over and you revert to your normal form, you will be as vulnerable as any wolf."

"I thought that was just in old movies," Charlie Loon said.

"Much of what is in the movies, the good ones, is true," Jack said. "At least the ones I've been consulted on." They all looked at the shaman in surprise. For all Egil knew, Jack was telling the truth and he had served as a consultant to the movies. Noting about his friend would surprise him at this point.

"That's beside the point, right now," Egil said. "Exactly what happened to you?"

"I was coming back from the lake. I'd been fishing. I heard some noise in the bushes. It sounded like maybe a half dozen men walking slowly and carefully, trying not to make any sound. Next thing I know one of them shouts 'There he is' and there were some shots. That's when they got me. I slinked out of there as best I could in man-shape and headed back here after I had lost them."

"Be glad you were in man-shape," Jack commented. "If you hadn't been, you'd probably be dead now."

"But what happens in a day or two? If what you say is true, once I'm a wolf they can kill me with no problem."

"We'll have to deal with them before that, then," Jack said solemnly.

"Is there anything else you can tell us about these men?" Egil asked.

"Like I said, there were maybe half a dozen of them. I'm not real good with numbers. They all had long guns, and pistols too, I think. And there was something funny about two of them. They didn't smell right."

"What did they smell like?" Jack asked quietly.

"I don't know. Like matches after you light them, I guess."

"Sulfur," Jack said. "You were right when you said they weren't all human. Two of these hunters are demons."

"Demons? How are we supposed to fight demons?" Charlie Loon asked.

"Demons have their weaknesses. They aren't supposed to be in this world. Their proper place is the half world. It takes a lot of energy for them to maintain a presence. It upsets the balance of things. Nature wants to restore the balance. All it needs is a little help which we can give it. That still will leave the four normal men, but I think they won't remain if their backers are forced back into the half world."

"Ok. What do we do to restore the balance?"

"First, we must make some preparations. But we need to act quickly. If it is to be done, it should be done before the moon sets."

"We've got about three hours, then," White Eagle said, but Jack was already removing items from his bag.

He brought out a small drum and beater, a turtle shell rattle, and a long, hatchet shaped pipe which had a raven feather suspended from the bowl. Egil had never seen any of this apparatus before, but then he had rarely seen Jack operate in the persona of a Native American shaman. His own formal training had been mainly in classical European and Norse magics. CalThaum had not been strong on the indigenous aspects of the Art.

"Can either of you drum?" Jack asked Charlie and John.

Charlie replied, "My grandfather taught me some."

Jack handed the drum and beater to him. For some reason he handed the rattle to Egil. From out of his pack, Jack pulled a fur pelt. Egil thought it looked like wolf. He looked at his client. The latter wrinkled his nose and said, "coyote." Jack draped the pelt over his shoulders so that the front paws hung down on his breast. Finally, he took a small pouch of tobacco and filled the bowl of the pipe.

"Are we ready? I need to make the chant to the four winds." Charlie Loon took this as a cue and began a slow beat on the drum. Jack began to chant in a low voice. Carefully, he lit the bowl of the pipe. Then, still chanting, he faced to the north. Egil wasn't sure how he did it, but Jack always seemed to have an unerring sense of direction. For no other reason than it seemed like a good idea, Egil began to shake the rattle in time to the drum.

Jack paused to take a puff on the pipe. He held the smoke a long time and then expelled it in a large cloud to the north. He continued the chant turning counterclockwise to face the west. He repeated the procedure. The tiny room of the cabin seemed to be getting much hazier than the amount of smoke the pipe produced warranted. Egil noticed that John White Eagle was echoing Jack's chant, maintaining the cadence while Jack inhaled the smoke from the pipe. Again the shaman turned, this time to the south. He inhaled, held the smoke for a moment and then blew it out again. His form was starting to become indistinct, as if he was half one thing and half another. Egil wondered if there was something more than tobacco in the pipe.

Finally, Jack turned and faced the east. Once more he took a pull on the pipe, held the smoke, and breathed out. When he had finished, he was no longer Jack. Instead he had taken on the appearance of a creature, half man, half animal, as if he were a coyote standing on two legs.

He handed the pipe and tobacco pouch to John White Eagle. "Do not let it go out until the moon sets." The latter nodded as if he understood the importance.

Jack opened the gun case that he had brought and pulled out a spear. The case was only about three feet long, but the spear was at least six feet long and tipped with a leaf-shaped stone blade. Egil had seen such stone spear points before, in museums where they were labeled Clovis. Not for the first time he wondered just how old his friend actually was.

Taking the spear in his hand, Jack flung the door open and disappeared into the night.

"He's become Coyote," Charlie Loon said, still maintaining the beat on the drum. "My grandfather told me about how some shamans could do that, but I never believed him."

Egil knew enough Native American lore to know that Coyote was a central figure in their mythology. Coyote, the trickster, was a being similar to the Norse Loki, but not inherently evil as Loki was. Whatever his motivation, Coyote was an immensely powerful spirit. Nothing in his training had prepared him for this, for he had a feeling that his friend Jack had not just created an illusion, but that he had, in some way, actually become or invoked the presence of Coyote.

The four of them stood in the smoke filled cabin. Subconsciously, they had each taken up the position of one of the four compass points around the flame of the kerosene lantern. Charlie Loon kept up his drumming, Egil repeated it with the rattle. Periodically, John White Eagle would take a pull of smoke from the pipe and puff it out into the room. The man-wolf stood at his point, eyes wide.

Out in the woods, they could hear that the wind had risen. Occasionally, there would be a shout or a cry from one of the hunters. Except, now they had become the hunted as Coyote led them on his merry chase. Periodically, shots echoed through the forest. The cabin had only one small window, the glass dark from years of dirt, but they could see the gun flashes, first up close, then far away, then nearer again. A shot rang out, then the cry of a man, wounded.

The moon was drawing closer to the horizon. Through the west facing window they could see it just above the tree tops. Still they kept up the beat. There was another shot and a cry, then a third. It now sounded as if only three hunters were active.

Another cry of a wounded man. The moon was now behind the trees, producing a ghostly silhouette. The cries of the hunters were no longer human, but Egil could hear the frustration and anger in those demon voices. They were no match for the power of Coyote.

Finally, the moon had sunk below the horizon. No beam pierced the screen of trees. The forest had gone silent. Not even the normal night sounds could be heard. All animal life had long ago sought shelter from the magical battle that had been going on in those dark woods.

As if by common assent, Charlie Loon stopped his drumming and Egil silenced his rattle. John White Eagle placed the cold pipe on the table next to the lantern. They stood in silence for long minutes, then the door opened.

It was Jack, now just a man with an animal skin draped over his shoulders.

"Egil, me lad," Jack asked in his best Irish brogue. "You wouldn't have any more of that Tullamore dew about you, would you. It's been a long and thirsty night."

Egil pulled a flask out of his jacket pocket and handed it to the wizard.

"Are they gone?" John White Eagle asked.

"The demons are gone. They won't be back, either. The men—well the bodies are out there. One or two might even still be alive. Somehow in the confusion they managed to shoot each other."

"So things are back to normal?" Charlie Loon queried.

"The balance has been restored, if that's what you mean," Jack responded.

"Not quite," the wolf said. "What about me? I still don't want to be a man."

"I haven't forgotten you," Jack said. "I've an idea how the curse might be lifted. But that's a job for another night. Right now I need some breakfast and then a long days sleep."

It was nearly a month later, on the night of the full moon, that Egil and Jack returned to Wolf Lake. During the intervening time, Jack had refused to divulge what he had planned, but on the drive up he given some hints as to what he had in mind.

"It's a question of balance. It came to me while I was running around the woods in the persona of Coyote. Native American beliefs are all about maintaining a balance in nature. When nature is out of balance, bad things happen. That was how I was able to dispel the demons. Their presence in this world destroyed the balance and took an enormous amount of energy. All it took was a little push and that energy drained off and the demons were returned to the half world.

"Now creating a were-creature, of whatever sort, alters the balance of nature. When Bad Moon cursed your client, it created an imbalance. Normally, to undo a curse, you have to know the nature of the curse, or convince the person who authored the curse to undo it. In this case, because of the demise of Bad Moon, neither is possible. He was into some very powerful magics, magics that even I am unfamiliar with."

"So how can we help my client?"

"Well that's where Coyote comes in. This is essentially a problem between the Wolf Lake people and the wolf. Western, or even Eastern methods don't apply. What is needed is to restore the balance between the Wolf Lake Band and the wolf."

"And how do you propose to go about doing that."

"I'm thinking something in terms of a ceremony. A meeting if you will between the members of the Wolf Lake Band and the wolf under a full moon where the band asks for the forgiveness of the wolf and the wolf grants it."

"And you think that will do it?" Egil asked skeptically.

"That's what I'm hoping. And even if it doesn't, I think bringing it out into the open will help to restore the balance so that they all can live in peace."

When they got to Wolf Lake, they drove first to the wolf's cabin to pick him up, and then to the small casino run by the tribe. It took a bit of persuading to get the wolf to accompany them, but when he understood the purpose, he agreed. John White Eagle had arranged, according to Jack's instructions, to gather all four hundred some members of the Wolf Lake Band at the casino.

It was really a very picturesque sight that greeted them at the casino. The casino occupied an old lodge on the lake which had a large lawn big enough to accommodate the gathering. A large fire burned in the center of the lawn, and a few of the older members of the band were off to one side beating on a large drum while some of the younger members dressed in traditional costume danced around the fire. The rest of the band stood around in small groups talking to each other, minding the children or just watching.

They had timed it so that they arrived about ten minutes before midnight, that is midnight by the moon, and not daylight savings time. Jack, Egil, and the wolf approached the fire where John White Eagle and Charlie Loon stood.

"Are you ready?" White Eagle asked.

"Ready as I'll ever be," Jack responded.

"All right then," White Eagle said nervously. "Everybody! Can I get your attention?"

The drummers and dancers stopped and a hush came over the crowd. In the distance frogs could be heard and off across the lake came the cry of a loon.

"You all know that for a while some strange things have been happening around here, ending up with that business last month. Well, we've brought you all together to put an end to it. I don't really understand these things very well, so I've asked Charlie Loon to explain it."

Charlie Loon moved forward a couple of steps. "I don't know that I understand these things any better than John, but here goes. A while back Harold Bad Moon put a curse on a wolf. That was the night he got drunk and drowned himself. Anyway, he cursed this wolf so that every full moon this wolf becomes a man. Now that might not seem so bad, but the wolf doesn't want to be a man. He just wants to be a wolf all the time, which is only natural and right.

"Well, Harold Bad Moon was a member of our band. He was our shaman, and so, even if we didn't ask him to do it, we all, as the Wolf Lake Band, are at fault for this wolf's problems. And this curse had put things out of whack. So to restore the balance we, each and every one of us, has got to ask the wolf's pardon, ask him to forgive us, and maybe if we all do that and he forgives us, the curse will be lifted and the balance restored.

"This fella here," he said indicating the wolf, "is the wolf. Some of you may know him as John Wolfe, but he's really a wolf." This caused a lot of murmuring as not everyone believed the whole story.

"Anyway, this old man here," indicating Jack, "is a powerful shaman. Believe me, I've seen him at work. He says this is the right thing to do, so now is the time for each of us to step up and ask the wolf's forgiveness. Wolf, I'm sorry this happened, it was wrong and I want to make it right."

John White Eagle then spoke up and said, "Wolf, I'm sorry."

There was a moment of silence then an old woman who looked to be about ninety came forward and looked the wolf in the eye and said, "Wolf, I'm sorry."

After that, each member of the band came forward and asked the wolf's forgiveness. When they had all spoken and there were no more coming forward, the wolf stepped out and said, "I know that this wasn't your fault. I don't hold a grudge against the Wolf Lake people. Whether this works or not, I forgive you all."

With that, Jack came up an whispered in the wolf's ear. The wolf began to undress in front of the entire group. Jack looked up at the moon as if to judge the exact moment of midnight. The instant he looked down again the wolf's form began to flow and alter. No longer was he a man, but he had become that which was his nature, a wolf.

The long grey form started to walk towards the forest. The Wolf Lake people parted before him. He walked, not slinked, slowly and confidently. When he reached the edge of the woods he looked back once, and then disappeared into the forest. A little while later there came a long howl from deep in the woods, but it was not a howl of longing, it was a howl of being.

"That's done then, is it?" Charlie Loon asked when the howl had died off.

"I believe so," Jack said. "I think the curse is lifted and the wolf will remain a wolf always."

"Well, after tonight, I don't think any of our people will complain about wolves taking deer or elk. Not around here," John White Eagle said. "On behalf of the Wolf Lake Band I'd like to thank you two for all your help. And if you ever want to come up for a bit of fishing, I know all the best spots."

They shook hands, then Jack said, "I can't keep coming up here every time there's trouble. It's too far. I've know a shaman in the neighborhood. I've talked it over with him and he's agreed to handle all your normal medicine work. Here's his card." He handed a business card to Charlie Loon.

"Come on, Egil, time to get back to civilization." Jack said before heading to the car.

Sneak Preview

From the book

Star City Stories

Space Opera Noir
Featuring Frank Sladek, P.I.

By Greg Fowlkes

Ray-Guns on Star City

The Blue Moon was different than other bars on Star City. It was dark and cool. But mostly it was quiet. There wasn't any sound projector blaring the latest jive samba. There weren't any holocasters spewing pitches for products no one needed. There wasn't even a televisor showing sporting events except for during the Worlds Series. That's one of the reasons I liked the place.

Mostly though, I go there because it's across the street from where I live, a not too crummy apartment building on the fringes of New Minglewood. New Minglewood is the district of Star City where the grifters, whores and all the other low-lifes with no regular employment live. They live there because the rent is cheap. Also it's the only place that will have them.

Star City was built on a hunk of rock that failed as a planet. Once a fortnight it orbits around a star that never made it to the big time, but is doomed to spend eternity as a brown dwarf stuck in the middle of nowhere. There's no reason at all for Star City to exist except that it happens to be at the place where a half dozen space routes intersect making it a convenient place for transshipments and for making connections. When they discovered it, they hollowed it out, spun it up to give it the semblance of gravity it could never generate on its own, and built a pair of docking rings at each end. They can handle a hundred ships at a time, and there are always a dozen more parked in orbit waiting a berth.

Half the commerce of human space passes through Star City, and with it comes half the population, or at least so it seems. Star City has grown up catering to the needs and whims of those travelers making a layover whether they are moguls or deck hands. You can buy any sort of food or beverage known. You can find entertainment to pass the time until your ship leaves. You can gamble a fortune away at a dozen casinos; or bet your last dollar.

Me, I was nursing a whiskey and soda in the middle of the afternoon. I knew it was whiskey because it was brown and ninety proof. If it had been clear it would have been gin or vodka. In either case, it had never been within a light year of Scotland or Tennessee or any other place on any respectable planet circling a real sun. I was drinking in the middle of the afternoon because I didn't have anything better to do.

I was alone in the place except for the bartender and one other customer who sat at the far end with a stack of Crockett dollars piled up on the bar in front of him. Every fifteen minutes the barkeep would bring him a shot of something blue and remove two dollar coins from the pile. He never seemed to take the empty glasses away. There looked to be about a dozen.

The guy was nondescript looking, about middle age, middle height, middle weight. He looked like he might be a travelling salesman. There was something that looked like it might be a sample case resting on the floor next to his barstool. He was leaning on the bar staring into space. In that position it was hard to tell if he was drunk or just weary of the world. He'd looked up for a minute when I had walked in, but after giving me the once-over returned to contemplating the blue liquid in the shot glass in front of him.

The bartender knew me well enough to know that I wasn't interested in conversation. The salesman wasn't talking, either. That suited the bartender just fine as it gave him plenty of time to polish glasses with the dirty rag he kept tucked in his belt.

It was almost with annoyance that he looked up when the door opened to accept a new denizen of the bar. This guy was anything but ordinary. Just shy of two meters tall he was wearing a flash suit that looked as if it cost what the average Joe made in a month. He had what is euphemistically called a "spacer tan." Of course, real spacers never see the light of a sun and are normally pale as ghosts. I was thinking he was in the wrong bar in the wrong part of Star City.

He walked up to the bar and motioned for the bartender. Like he needed to attract attention when there were only two other customers in the place.

"I'm looking for a woman. Tall, good-looking, red hair. She's wearing a black dress cinched at the waist and black, high-heeled boots. Has she been in here?"

"Sorry mister," the bartender said. "There ain't been no woman looking like that in here all day, and my shift started at eight." Truth was there hadn't been any woman in there all day, and certainly not one like he had described.

"You sure? She said she'd meet me here."

"Nope. No one like that in here today. You want a drink while you wait?"

"No, I'll pass. Are there any other bars named the Blue Moon on Star City?"

"Not that I know of. There is a Red Planet Saloon down by the spacedocks, but I wouldn't go there. It's a dive from what I hear." I knew the place. The bartender was right. The Red Planet was definitely not a place to go looking for a good-looking red head. Or for anything else unless it was trouble.

"Thanks. If she comes in here, tell her I was here."

"Who shall I say?"

"She'll know who."

He turned and headed for the door. The guy at the other end of the bar stood up, his hand reaching inside his jacket. For a wonder he didn't fall down. He called out, "Yano!"

The guy at the door turned to face him, a look of concern on his face. There were what sounded like three soft sneezes and suddenly three red spots appeared on his chest just where his heart would be. He looked for a moment stunned and then he slumped to the floor.

I looked towards the guy at the end of the bar. He was holding a needle gun in his right hand. It was an assassin's weapon, small and quiet, firing tiny darts at hypersonic speeds. I knew then that he was no salesman.

I raised my hands to show I was unarmed. Frankly, I didn't think there was a chance in hell of my getting out of their alive, but even if I had been packing heat I knew I couldn't beat him. Not if he could place three darts within a circle smaller than a fist at ten meters in a dimly lit bar. The barkeep took his clue from me and raised his hands as well, the look of fear on his face.

The salesman/assassin scooped up the pile of Crockett dollars from the bar leaving two as a tip. That gave me some hope unless he had a twisted sense of humor. He stuffed the coins in his jacket pocket, then picked up his case with the same hand. All this time he was holding the needle gun in his right pointed nowhere in particular. He strode nonchalantly towards the door, stepping around the body. As he reached the door the needle gun disappeared into his jacket. Then he was gone.

"Holy Shiva! Mathew, Mark, George, and Ringo! What do we do now?"

The barkeep's theology might be confused, but I shared his sentiment.

"I suggest we wait ten minutes, then you call the cops," I said, trying to sound calm and like I knew what I was doing. I wasn't either.

"You going to be here then?" he asked.

"No reason not to. I still got some of my drink left."

I waited five and then poked my nose out the door, looking both ways up and down the street. There was no sign of an assassin with a sample case. No red head in a black dress either. I ducked back into the bar.

"You might as well call the cops, now," I said, resuming my place at the bar.

From the Wizard at Law Series by Greg Fowlkes

The Laws of Magic

Egil Njalsson was an aspiring lawyer. A lawyer with a difference. Not only had he passed the bar, but he had an undergraduate degree from the most prestigious school of magic in the country, the California Institute of Thaumaturgy. Needless to say his caseload and clients tended to the unusual. Like witches; or vampires. And the opposition, well they were likely to be demons. But Egil Njalsson had sworn an oath to uphold the law of the land, and... *The Laws of Magic*!

Trial By Magic

Egil Njalsson is just another practicing attorney. Except, that is, for the occasional unusual client. Such as the ghost who retained his services using e-mail. Or the wolf who has been cursed by an Indian shaman to turn into a human during the full moon. Or the Leprechaun who is facing the loss of his saloon. Even when the clients are human, they have unusual problems like the Creole chef accused of making a rival a zombie or the scientist accused of transmuting a man into a statue of silicon. Yet somehow, Egil manages to resolve all his client's problems whether legal or magical. Of course it helps that he is a wizard as well as a lawyer.

Trial by Magic includes five new tales from the same world as *The Laws of Magic*.

From the Murder on Mars Series by Greg Fowlkes

Blood Reds Sands of Mars

On Mars the wind was rising. The grains of sand could be heard abrading the thin aluminum skin that was the only protection against the outside. On the far side of Olympus Mons a prospector lies dead in the sand. Inspector Erik McKernan, head of the handful of men that make up the small Martian police force must find the killer while threading the maze of corporate and international politics that govern the planet, and he must do it while trying to survive . . .*The Blood Red Sands of Mars!*

A Death at Station Alpha

Station Alpha, a remote Martian research facility isolated by a planet wide dust storm. When one of the scientists is found murdered, it falls to Inspector McKernan to determine which of the remaining twelve people at the station wielded the fatal weapon. But, as the crime was committed in a locked laboratory with no possible access and all the suspects would seem to have unbreakable alibis, it will take all his skills as a detective to solve the puzzle of *A Death at Station Alpha*. Thirty years in the making, the long awaited sequel to *The Blood Red Sands of Mars*.

A Corpse in Hut Town

Hut Town is the remnants of the original Martian settlement; a collection of inflatable buildings abandoned by the Trust Authority and the mining corporations and now occupied by those catering to the baser needs of miners and construction workers in for a spree. But when a corpse is found in one of the service tunnels, Chief Inspector McKernan is called in.

He has plenty of questions. Who's body is it? How did they die? How did they get to Mars in the first place, and why weren't they missed? And the most important one on the Inspector's mind— are there any more bodies down there?

Murder at the Mars Club

The Mars Club was the sanctuary of the rich and powerful on Mars, so when one of the members is found dead, Chief Inspector is called in to solve the case as discretely as possible. Will the solution of the case prove to be the one man he'd least like to implicate?

From the Fictional Detective Series by Greg Fowlkes

The Fictional Detective

Mystery writer Ezekial O. Handler has been killed in a suspicious car crash. Private detective Frank Slade has been hired by Handler's beautiful girlfriend to investigate. Handler, seemingly with a premonition of his death, has left a trail of clues. Can Slade discover the murderer, or will he instead uncover a secret that will shake his existence to the core?

A Fictional Detective Trifecta

The Fictional Detective has gotten out of the Private Investigator game. Instead, he's trying to write hard-boiled masterpieces such as *Death Buys a Condo*. But despite the fact that the door of his office now says WRITER, some of his clients haven't gotten the word. And a strange lot of clients they are. A man that only contacts him during séances because, well, he's dead; a female impersonator who has inherited a house that's just a little too haunted for the market, and a small time gambler who's trying to end an affair with Lady Luck.

Three All New Novellas featuring the Fictional Detective!

SPACE OPERA NOIR!

STAR CITY STORIES: SPACE OPERA NOIR FEATURING FRANK SLADEK
BY GREG FOWLKES

The mean streets of Star City, a hollowed out asteroid circling a failed star in the middle of nowhere breed a special sort of man. With grifters, hoodlums, and two-bit con-men from every planet In human space trying to make the big score, it takes someone like Frank Sladek, sometime private detective, sometime finder of lost items, to navigate the maze of corruption and double-crosses that is Star City. As quick with his wit as with a needler or laser pistol, Sladek can handle anyone, except maybe the dames. These are just a few of the Star City Stories.

Books by Greg Fowlkes

From the Wizard at Law Series:

The Laws of Magic
Trial by Magic

From the Murder on Mars Series:

Blood Red Sands of Mars
A Death at Station Alpha
A Corpse in Hut Town
Murder at the Mars Club

From the Fictional Detective Series:

The Fictional Detective
A Fictional Detective Trifecta

Star City Stories: Space Opera Noir Featuring Frank Sladek

The Uncorrupted Corpse

Tequila Visions

Cargo From Paradise

Ice Viking

The Fictional Press
www.TheFictionalPress.com

The Fictional Press is an imprint of Intrepid Ink, LLC. Find out more at www.TheFictionalPress.com.

About Intrepid Ink, LLC

Intrepid Ink, LLC provides full publishing services to authors of fiction and non-fiction books, eBooks and websites. From editing to formatting, from publishing to marketing, Intrepid Ink gets your creative works into the hands of the people who want to read them. Find out more at www.IntrepidInk.com.